D0481076

END
of the
WORLD

LLYFRGELLOEDD ABERTAWE
SWANSEA LIBRARIES

4000003484

the Bus Stop at the END of the WORLD

Ritchie says that almost everything that happens in this story is true.

Gomer

Published in 2017 by Gomer Press, Llandysul,
Ceredigion SA44 4JL
www.gomer.co.uk

ISBN 978 1 78562 199 4
ISBN 978 1 78562 200 7 (EPub)
ISBN 978 1 78562 201 4 (Kindle)

A CIP record for this title is available from the British Library.

© text: Dan Anthony, 2017
© illustrations: Huw Aaron, 2017

Dan Anthony and Huw Aaron have asserted their moral right
under the Copyright, Designs and Patents Act, 1988 to be
identified as author and illustrator of this work.

All rights reserved. No part of this book may be reproduced,
stored in a retrieval system, or transmitted in any form
or by any means, electronic, electrostatic, magnetic tape,
mechanical, photocopying, recording or otherwise without
permission in writing from the above publishers.

This book is published with the financial support of the
Welsh Books Council.

Printed and bound in Wales at
Gomer Press, Llandysul, Ceredigion

1 The red sweet

EVERY DAY Jamie gave Ritchie a red sweet. Ritchie couldn't remember exactly when the habit started. Now, if it was a school day, his dad wouldn't let him leave the house without handing him a red sweet and Ritchie wouldn't go without taking one.

Ritchie made his way from the cottage down the Winding Lane, sucking the sweet. When he reached the end of the lane he crossed the Big Road and stood in the bus stop. He let the sweet slide around his mouth as he scanned the empty road stretching away into the Boggy Hills for a glimpse of the 971. There was no bus. He was early. He closed his eyes and concentrated on the sweet in his mouth. He inched the tip of his tongue along the bumps in its surface. It felt like a giant rock with craters on. It felt like the moon in his mouth.

Suddenly, Ritchie was disturbed by a pat on the back.

Ritchie spun around. He hadn't seen or heard anyone arrive at the bus stop, nobody ever did. Ritchie's bus stop was in the middle of nowhere. On one side of the road the fields sloped gently down to the cliffs and the sea and on the other they went up, past the cottage and the farm to the Old Mountains. He was the only one who ever caught a bus from that stop.

A man wearing old pin-striped trousers, a big belt, a check shirt and a wide brimmed hat spoke to him. 'You look like a good boy,' he said.

Ritchie coughed and choked, the pat on the back had made him swallow his red sweet.

'But are you?' asked the man, staring at the distant cliffs where the ferry was nosing its way out into the blue sea, as if it was looking for something.

'What d'you mean?' asked Ritchie.

'The kind of boy who keeps his eyes open, his ears to the ground and makes observations,' replied the man with a wink.

'I'm not much good in school, if that's what you mean,' said Ritchie.

'I see you have the uniform,' said the man,

looking at Ritchie's new Year 7 school sweatshirt. 'That's something.'

Ritchie stared back at the man. He was maybe a bit older and a bit shorter than his dad. He had thick bushy eyebrows, big dark brown eyes, a fat black moustache, and stubble on his chin like black pepper on rice pudding. He looked like a cowboy.

'This is a fine spot you've chosen,' said the man.

Ritchie shrugged his shoulders. He hadn't really chosen the bus stop. He supposed it had chosen him. Where else was he supposed to catch the bus to school?

'Do you catch the bus every day?' asked the man.

'Every day,' replied Ritchie. 'Sometimes I just come down here anyway.'

'Why do you do that?' asked the man.

'I dunno,' said Ritchie. 'I like it here. I know loads of the bus drivers. And the times. I know the times of the planes too.'

'Good,' said the man, glancing upwards at the vapour trails that the passenger jets made in the blue, spring sky. 'I want you to do me a favour.'

'What?' asked Ritchie, picking up his plastic bag; he could see the sunlight flashing off the sky-blue roof of the 971 in the distance as it edged its way down Second Hill.

'I have to go now. But I have a friend – taller than me, he wears a liquorice tie and boots with Cuban heels,' said the man. 'Do you know what a Cuban heel is?'

'No,' said Ritchie.

'They're big, and the boots are pointy,' explained the man.

'A real cowboy, not like you,' said Ritchie.

'His name is Doc – Doc Penfro. Check him out, ask him his name.'

The bus was getting closer.

'I've got to get on this bus; I can't hang around here listening to you.'

'Tell him you met me and I gave you this message,' said the man.

'Who are you? What's the message?' asked Ritchie, shifting nervously from foot to foot. He could see the bus clearly now – it had reached the top of the First Hill and was speeding down towards his stop. It was almost time for him to put his hand out.

'Tell him that they have arrived,' said the man. 'And tell him you met Kid.'

Ritchie stuck his hand out and waved at the bus. He didn't know whether the bus would stop for him if he didn't stick his hand out. He wasn't going to risk that. The next bus along would be the 872 to Haverfordwest. It didn't go anywhere near his school.

The bus slowed down and stopped and the driver, Mr Dickinson, greeted him with a friendly blast on his horn. 'Morning, Ritchie,' he shouted as the pneumatic doors hissed open. Ritchie stepped on, turning to speak to the man with the message.

But as the doors slapped shut Ritchie couldn't see him. It was as if he had not been there.

2 Annie Bike

RITCHIE STEPPED off the bus at half past four. He'd been talking to Gloria Harris; she often drove the evening school bus. Ritchie always sat at the front. He liked to see all the things the drivers could. He liked to watch the speedo on the dashboard; he liked looking in the mirrors and he liked to keep an eye on the road, imagining that his own hands were controlling the big steering wheel. The route was the 971 but the actual bus number was 24, which meant that it was number 24 in the Williams Brothers' fleet. It was a Volvo City Bus. They usually put it on the Swansea run, but it had been diverted because the normal country bus, number 37, was in for a service. Ritchie always made it his business to ask the drivers what was happening at the depot.

'See you tomorrow, boy,' shouted Gloria, as Ritchie jumped off.

He watched as the 971 roared away up the First Hill. Ritchie didn't feel like walking back up the Winding Lane to the cottage. He crossed the road to the bus stop and started playing with stones on the ground. It was a sunny afternoon. The fields around him were full of fattening lambs and the hedgerows were just beginning to sprout with spring leaves and flowers. Above him he could see the trails of the jets streaking across the blue sky from London to America, all zooming along the Strumble Head flight path, out past Ireland and then off over the Atlantic Ocean. Strumble Head, the place that the jet pilots used to work out where Britain ended and the sea started, was where Ritchie's bus stop stood. Ritchie's bus stop was underneath one of the busiest flight paths in the world, in the middle of nowhere in the far west of West Wales. Inside the bus stop it was as warm as a greenhouse; Ritchie sat on the floor to play with the stones.

He was disturbed by the screeching of breaks. It was Annie, the girl from the farm where he and his dad had their cottage, pulling up on her bike.

'What you doing, Ritchie?' asked Annie Bike.

Ritchie looked out from inside the bus stop. 'Nothing, really.'

'Funny kind of nothing,' said Annie stepping off her bike and into the bus stop. She stared down at the pieces of gravel on the concrete floor. She could see there was some kind of pattern to them.

'You playing with stones?' she asked.

Ritchie shrugged. He hated being found out; he knew he was too old to play like a kid. 'No,' he said. 'So?' he asked.

Annie put her foot on the pebbles, which Ritchie had carefully arranged opposite the flakes of grit and tarmac.

Annie was older than Ritchie. She'd been living on the farm all her life and knew everything and everybody. Ritchie had only been in the cottage for a few months. Annie never went on the bus; she went everywhere on her bike. Ritchie was in Year 7. Annie was in Year 9.

'Who are these?' she asked, moving her foot from the little white smooth pebbles back to the gritty stuff.

'They're the insurgents,' explained Ritchie.

'What's an insurgent?' asked Annie.

'The Taliban,' said Ritchie. He nodded at the pebbles. 'That's Camp Bastion. We're in there.'

Annie looked down at Ritchie and smiled. 'You're mad, you are.'

Ritchie knelt on the floor and put the pebbles back in the right places. 'Don't smash it up,' he said.

'Why would I do that?' asked Annie, walking out the bus stop, swinging her leg over her saddle. 'Wanna lift home?'

'No, it's OK ,' replied Ritchie.

'Suit yourself,' said Annie. 'See you tomorrow.'

Annie rode off. She was skinny and strong, and could go for miles on that bike.

Ritchie sat on the floor in the bus stop and began moving the pebbles around. When he was satisfied that his troops were positioned properly he stood up, brushed the dust off his trousers and walked out onto the roadside.

The sun was dropping low in the west and the temperature was falling. All around, Ritchie could hear the birds roosting in the trees and bushes. They sounded like a fire crackling. A crow flapped over and perched on top of the bus stop. Ritchie had noticed the bird before. It seemed to like the bus stop.

'What you looking at?' asked Ritchie. The next bus, the 479 to Cardigan, wouldn't be there for another hour. It was OK to talk out loud. There was nobody around to laugh at him.

The crow turned its head and looked away.

'Don't talk to crows,' said a soft voice.

Ritchie jumped. He spun around. Somehow he must have missed the lady in the woolly brown coat with the woolly brown hat standing next to the stone field boundary near the metal gate. She stepped forward, out of the lengthening shadows.

'I haven't seen you before,' she said.

'I haven't seen you either,' said Ritchie, thinking that there were suddenly an awful lot of people visiting his bus stop. He knew for sure that this lady, who seemed to be nothing more than a woollen coat under a knitted hat, hadn't been at the bus stop before.

'I'm waiting for the 479,' she explained.

'It won't be here for another hour,' said Ritchie, crossing the road.

'Wait one moment,' said the woman.

Ritchie stepped back off the empty road and onto the grass patch next to the bus stop.

'That crow,' said the woman in the coat.

She turned her head towards it. 'Don't say anything to it.'

'Why not?' asked Ritchie.

'Just don't. The less the crow knows, the better.'

Ritchie nodded, then he crossed the road and walked to the Winding Lane with its high hawthorn hedges sprouting out of stone boundaries. When he was sure she couldn't see him, he ran home.

3 The green sweet

ON SATURDAYS Jamie didn't give Ritchie a red sweet. Jamie said it was unlucky for him not to give Ritchie something on 'no school' days. So he gave him a green sweet instead. Saturday always started with a green sweet. Ritchie thought it was like a green light, a sign that he was free from all the bad stuff in school.

Sometimes Jamie would take Ritchie into town and they'd go shopping and then to the pub where Jamie would drink beer and talk to Neville. Ritchie would sit by the window and drink glasses of coke and maybe play with Sheba, Neville's labrador. Neville ran the pub; sometimes he'd give Ritchie a bowl of chips, pretending that nobody had seen him steal them from the kitchen. Ritchie thought this was very funny, because Neville was only stealing the chips from himself.

On other Saturdays, Jamie would go to town on his own, leaving Ritchie to look after the house.

This week had been the worst so far. Ritchie never told Jamie about school, because he knew he'd blow his top. Only a few kids bullied him – the Collins gang, mainly. But that was OK, because Ritchie could usually tell where they'd be and just stay out of their way. He didn't really know the rest because he was new. The kids in his class all called him 'Ritchie Rich' – he didn't know why; nobody seemed to know who the real Ritchie Rich was. If anything came up in a lesson and they didn't know the answer they'd say: 'We dunno – ask Ritchie Rich!' And the teacher, thinking that this was a good joke, would ask Ritchie and he'd say what he thought and the teacher would smile and say that it was wrong or just plain weird. And then they'd all laugh. Sometimes Ritchie laughed too, because he didn't know whether he should or he shouldn't. Nothing really funny ever happened in school.

On Friday he'd been put in with Miss Croons' literacy group, for extra help with his reading. He'd have to go there instead of Art with Miss Morgan, the only lesson he really liked. When he got back to class, Connor Collins said that Ritchie couldn't even read his own name and everyone laughed again.

Jamie had gone to town; Ritchie reached the end of the Winding Lane. This time Ritchie took a good look around before he stepped out of the lane. He stuck his head out from behind the stone field boundary and watched the road. It was empty. He sucked on the sweet. There was nobody around. The tarmac lay like a silent river in front of him. Ritchie crossed the road and stepped into the bus stop. He'd left it like this; the troops were arranged in defensive positions for night duty. Most of his forces were inside Camp Bastion, arranged in a neat square. Dotted around, on high ground and in slip trenches, he'd put his best snipers with night gear. Just outside the camp he'd stationed some armoured vehicles, camouflaged and hidden, but ready to go in case of a surprise attack. The insurgents were spread out in the hills and fields around. They were concentrating on drawing his troops out of the camp and weren't about to mount a big frontal attack.

But when Ritchie stepped into the bus stop and looked at the stones on the ground, he saw something abnormal had happened. The stones were all mixed up into a pattern. It looked like the swirl of a snail's shell, the white pebbles in the middle and the sharp stones on the edge. Someone had moved the stones. As Ritchie put them back exactly as they were, the crow returned. Ritchie could see it perched on the opposite side of the road and always seemed to have its eye on him. Ritchie spoke to his men; he told them to get back into formation.

'Did you see anything?' he asked.

The crow watched.

'I bet it was that old lady in the woolly coat,' muttered Ritchie. 'The Woolly Woman.'

He went to find some sticks. As he rummaged around by the gate to the field he noticed the sheep and their lambs in the field. One of them, a black one, seemed to be watching him, just like the crow. It moved towards him. In the end, the sheep was so close to Ritchie he could have stuck his hand through the metal railings and patted him on the nose. That wasn't unusual; Ritchie spent such a lot of time at the bus stop that the animals had got used to him. He'd watched lots of the lambs being born out in the field. Once he'd noticed a pregnant ewe lying on the grass bleating – crying, he thought – and a couple of the other mothers had come and stood with her. So he'd run up to the farm to get Annie's dad who'd come down and helped the sheep have her twins. He said Ritchie would make a good farmer. But Ritchie didn't want to be a farmer. He wanted to be a soldier.

Ritchie had collected a handful of good sticks. The black sheep chewed and watched him.

'D'you know anything about the crow?' asked Ritchie.

The sheep looked at him and then the crow, with his strange sideways-pointing eyes, sliding its mouth from side to side.

'The lady who moved my stones told me not to talk to him. How dumb is that? He's just a bird.'

The sheep moved a tiny bit closer, pressing his nose through the gate. His alien eyes seemed to X-ray Ritchie.

'I know,' said Ritchie, 'and you're just a sheep. Sorry.'

Then the black sheep did something strange. He stopped chewing and sniffed the ground. He picked up a little dead twig that had fallen from the hedge. He walked a step or two and dropped it out of his mouth. Then he found another twig and put it next to the first one, then another.

Ritchie watched the sheep. It seemed to him as if the sheep was trying to tell him something. It was making a pattern out the sticks, like the stones.

'Are you trying to talk?' gasped Ritchie.

The crow watched.

Ritchie was getting fed up with the crow.

A bus pulled up. The sheep trotted off and Ritchie hurried back to the stop with his sticks. He waved at the driver, Dave Morris, on the 772 to Haverfordwest. One person got off the bus. He was tall, he wore a cowboy hat and his boots had big heels. He carried a bag made of carpet with a metal clasp on it.

Dave gave Ritchie a toot on his horn and drove off. The man strode around the bus stop, then he stopped and stared out towards the sea.

'Mighty fine view you've got here, boy,' said the man, sucking in his cheeks as he filled his lungs with sea air. 'You can't beat the ozone of coastal community,' he said.

'Are you Doc Penfro?' asked Ritchie.

'Might be,' said the man, tipping his hat and looking down at Ritchie. 'Who's asking?'

'Ritchie,' said Ritchie.

ichard, huh?' said Doc.

ell, kind of,' said Ritchie. 'Is there a big one too?'

'Is this your bus stop?' asked the man.

'Kind of,' said Ritchie. He spotted the crow fluttering across the road and perching on the bus stop roof. Without thinking, Ritchie threw one of his sticks at the bird, causing it to flap further away. 'I've got a message,' he said quietly.

'I've got no time for games,' said the man, and he began walking away from the stop towards town, his carpet-bag swinging at his side.

'Wait,' shouted Ritchie.

The man stopped, turned slowly and retraced his steps. 'What's eatin' you, boy?'

'I've got a message from someone called Kid,' said Ritchie.

'Short legs, stupid hat, and a moustache like a brace of pigeons' wings?'

'Err, yeah, I think that's him,' said Ritchie.

'Kid Welly. I might have known he'd have got here first. What did he say?'

Ritchie looked around him. He checked the trees. The crow had settled a few hundred meters away in a little hawthorn tree, bent by the sea wind.

'I can't talk loud,' said Ritchie.

'Then talk quiet,' said Doc. He bent down, pushing his hat back on his head so that his face was close to Ritchie's. The bristles on his bony face stuck out like cactus spines, his breath was watery with the smell of canned beer.

'Kid says: "They have arrived",' said Ritchie.

Doc Penfro nodded. He drew himself up to his full height, looking gravely around the bus stop. 'Thanks, boy,' he said. 'Be seeing you.'

Doc began to walk away. Ritchie ran after him. 'Do you want me to do anything?' asked Ritchie.

'What's there to do?' Then, before striding off, Doc said: 'Well there is one thing, if you're really minded to help. If you see Kid Welly again, tell him I'm good for whatever he sees fit.'

Ritchie watched Doc disappear, the heels of his shiny boots clipping the tarmac. Then Ritchie remembered the sticks. He liked pushing them into the earth around the bus stop, and then he'd sit with his back to the outside of the bus stop and try and hit the sticks with pieces of gravel. It was target practice. It was no good getting close to a stick – you had to actually hit it before you could move on. Once you'd hit all the sticks it was OK to go home. It usually took hours to get the last, really difficult, target.

4 AWOL day

ON SUNDAYS, Jamie had made up a rule which meant it was an 'AWOL Day' – Absent Without Leave Day – so it didn't have to start with a sweet because anything could happen. It could be a bag of crisps, a toy – anything. This Sunday, as usual, there was Sunday roast in the General Picton. No matter how AWOL things became, there was always Sunday roast in the General Picton pub. Ritchie liked Sunday lunches. It was always a beef dinner with Yorkshire puddings and gravy in the General Picton. Jamie said that it didn't matter where you were in the world, you always had to have Sunday lunch. It was unlucky not to; it would be as mad as not having a red sweet or a green sweet.

The road was quiet. The crow pecked around the bus stop. A few cars slid slowly along the road.

From far away down near the town, a red Rover 45 appeared, crawling up the Steep Hill that rose up past the school and on to the bus stop. It came to a halt a little way before the bus stop, just before the Winding Lane. Inside the car, Jamie sat at the wheel singing along to one of the old tapes he played in the car's cassette player. Ritchie sat next to him. He didn't mind the ancient cassette player, but the tapes his dad liked drove him mad. The dashboard was littered with grimy old boxes with sun-bleached pictures of his dad's favourite: Elvis.

'Are you lonesome tonight?' screeched Jamie.

Ritchie tried to block it out. He hated Elvis Presley. His dad always sung his songs when he'd drunk too many cans. The noise was awful.

When they were in the pub having their Sunday roast, Ritchie had spotted Doc Penfro sitting alone at a table in the corner by the fire. On the next table a man kept telling a woman jokes and she laughed out loud, kicking his shoes with her sandals under the table. It was the boots Ritchie noticed. A little further away from the busy feet there were a pair of big Cuban heels. At first Ritchie hoped Doc hadn't seen him and he stuck close to his dad. But as Ritchie took a sneaky glance over, Doc raised his eyes from his bowl of cawl and winked. Ritchie made a face, shaking his head, trying to tell Doc not to come over and say hello. Doc nodded and dipped some bread in his food. That was a relief. His dad carried on talking, mainly about the army – telling Ritchie and Neville at the bar about all the weird and wonderful places where he and his mates had had Sunday lunches.

'We don't need anyone else, do we Ritchie boy?' Jamie had said as he wiped up his gravy with some bread. 'It's me and you against the world.'

Ritchie looked at his dad: his thinning crew cut, his too-tight green T-shirt, the three fading feathers inked on his forearm. Ritchie thought that if it really was him and his dad against everyone in the world, they were in for a bit of trouble. He tried to look happy.

'Yeah, Dad,' he said, in between mouthfuls of roast potatoes.

The car door opened, the oval wing mirror flashing in the sun, and Ritchie hopped out, full of beef dinner, ice cream and coke. The sound of Elvis flooded out over the road and all around the bus stop.

'Don't be late,' shouted Jamie, leaning across the empty passenger's seat, holding the door as Ritchie stepped out.

'You sure you don't want to watch the footy on the telly?' added his dad.

'Not really,' said Ritchie.

Ritchie looked at the bus stop.

'What do you do down here, Ritchie?' asked Jamie.

'Nothing, really,' said Ritchie.

The music stopped, Jamie ejected the tape, flipped it over and it started again. 'You can see why they call him the King of Rock 'n' Roll, can't you?' said Jamie.

'Not really,' replied Ritchie.

Jamie pulled the car door shut and turned across the road and up the little lane to their cottage.

Ritchie watched Jamie's Rover 45 hatchback – with 238,900 miles on the clock – disappear up the Winding Lane. The car was in perfect working order and there were hardly any rust spots. It was a great piece of engineering and it had been specially adapted for Jamie. Ritchie hated the way they laughed at their Rover on *Top Gear*. They made it out to be a bag of nails. But Ritchie knew it was a good car with a powerful engine that had never let them down. The number of miles on the clock of his dad's Rover was the same as the number of miles between the earth and the moon. Ritchie's Rover had driven as far away as the moon. Lamborghinis and Ferraris were good, too – but they weren't built to last as long as the Rover 45.

Ritchie walked to the bus stop. First he checked the stones. There were no patterns in the ground. He looked at the crow. The crow seemed sleepy. It flapped up onto the roof. Ritchie hurried to the gate, but all the sheep had been moved into another field.

Ritchie thought about his dad, and the fact that he hadn't told him about Doc Penfro and Kid Welly. His dad often got angry about things: about not being able to work, about not having any money and about what would happen to Ritchie if he didn't do better at school. Somehow, whatever Ritchie said would always end up with Jamie getting mad and swearing his head off about how unfair it all was. So Ritchie had learned to keep quiet.

The things that worried Ritchie were different to the ones that worried Jamie. For Jamie it was all about not having stuff: not having money; being left by Ritchie's mum; not having work; not having a fair chance; not having a new car; not having the luck he had when he was a soldier. For Ritchie these things were all fine: he loved their car; he didn't mind not having new clothes because he hated shopping anyway; he didn't even mind not having a mum, although he'd decided a while back that he wouldn't mind one, but he knew his dad kept himself to himself so there wasn't much chance of him getting another. Ritchie didn't miss his mum because he was so small when she left that he couldn't remember her. He liked helping his dad and he liked hanging around the bus stop; for him these were the easy bits.

Ritchie was worried about the big stuff – that's why he liked being on his own at the bus stop. Being on his own made him feel safe. For Ritchie, the things that worried him were simple. In the end they came down to one thing: he was a big disappointment for his dad.

He didn't have any friends, he was rubbish at football, and all his teachers thought he was a dead loss because he couldn't even read. The only thing he ever thought about in school was how best to get through the day without meeting the Collins gang. He was sure his dad wanted him to be better than he really was. Sometimes, when Jamie yelled at Ritchie, he felt that his dad thought that he was stuck with Ritchie as if, really, Ritchie was just another piece of bad luck. When this happened Ritchie went to the bus stop.

Ritchie sat in the bus stop and checked the Sunday timetable. There was only one bus due that afternoon – the 437 from Cardigan.

Ritchie tried not to think about school tomorrow. It was going to be terrible. He hadn't done his homework, his books were a mess and Connor Collins and his gang were going to beat him up if he didn't bring them some money. He didn't have any money and nor did his dad.

At first, Ritchie thought that the sound of breaking twigs was just the wind. Then he turned to look, thinking that maybe it was a sheep that had got caught up in some the wire at the edge of the field. He moved forward to get a closer look. He couldn't see anything unusual, then it became clearer. There was something in the brambles sprouting out of the stone field boundary. It took a second before Ritchie realised what the shape was. It was a human hand. Or rather, it was a bit like a human hand, flexing its short greenish fingers. It was horrible, like a fat, snaky spider. The hand pushed around and then Ritchie saw an arm and then a whole body, all mixed up with the hedge-wood. He shrank back into the bus stop, watching in horror as something slithered about in the hedge.

'It's not in here, blinkin' thing,' said the creature from the hedge.

With a great effort it pushed itself out of the hedge and rolled onto the floor. It was shaped like a man, but it was no bigger than Ritchie. It was wearing an old brown suit which was covered in earth, moss, twigs and grass. Its hair was wild, long and brown. Its eyes were different colours, one blue and one black. Its skin was olive-coloured green.

'Have you seen it?' asked the creature, picking earth out of its stubby fingernails with its yellow teeth.

Ritchie took another step back, shocked that the strange creature could speak. Although the creature looked nervous and jumpy, its voice was calm. It talked in a slow, deliberate way, in the kind of voice Annie's dad, the farmer, had – slow and careful.

'What?' asked Ritchie.

'The lost thing that I am looking for. It's here, there's no doubt about it. It's here at this intersection.'

Ritchie shook his head. He didn't understand what the creature was on about. It pulled itself up off the ground and its eyes flashed. Then, without blinking, it threw himself at Ritchie, knocking him to the floor. The creature was incredibly strong. In an instant it was sitting on Ritchie's chest, its huge hands squeezing Ritchie's neck. Ritchie could feel its skin – thick, like car tyres.

'The source – where's the blinkin' source?'

Ritchie, who was still quite sleepy after his lunch, looked around desperately. He wished he'd stayed with his dad. 'What source? What's a source?'

'You know the one I mean. You know!' said the creature, raising its voice.

Ritchie didn't know.

'I know you know,' hissed the creature, its eyes flashing with anger. 'Woody knows you know.'

'Who's Woody?' gasped Ritchie.

'I'm blinkin' Woody,' snapped the creature. 'Everybody knows Woody. I know you know. I can smell it here. I can feel it all around you and on you and in you. You're a One Off and no mistake. You're a blinkin' One Off. And *this* is the exact spot. *The* place.'

'Get off me,' shouted Ritchie, growing angry. He pushed his legs into the ground and shoved the creature with his chest as hard as he could.

The creature rolled on the floor and scuttled to his feet. He panted and snarled at Ritchie. Then he sniffed the air with his long nose.

'The power is here. Here is where it is. You are here and you are One Off. Where is it?'

'I don't know what you're talking about,' shouted Ritchie.

Ritchie was concentrating on Woody, trying to keep him in front of him so that he couldn't jump him. He could hear the bus coming up the hill. 'You hear that?'

'What?' hissed Woody.

'That's the 437 from Cardigan. It's a bus. I'll get the driver to radio the cops – then you're in big trouble.'

Woody stopped and watched the bus approaching. Mr Dickinson, the driver, tooted his horn.

'Blinkin' buses,' said Woody, 'I have to find the stone. I have to have the stone.'

'Go away,' shouted Ritchie. 'Get lost.'

Woody took one last look at the bus, then he threw himself into the hedge and began digging into the branches with his hands. In seconds he was gone, just like a fish disappearing into the sea. Ritchie listened to the rattling hedge as Woody scuttled away.

The doors of the bus hissed open. Ritchie spun around. The only people who lived up near the Winding Lane on the First Hill were him and his dad, Annie Bike and her mum and dad. Nobody got off the 437 on Sundays ever. But now two people did: a tall thin woman in a black suit, followed by mean-looking girl of about seventeen, carrying a big black handbag.

The driver tooted his horn and waved at Ritchie. Ritchie almost forgot to wave back.

'Who are you?' he asked, forgetting himself.

'What kind of a question is that, boy?' said the tall woman, pushing her white hair into shape. She held out her hand. The girl rummaged inside her bag, her beady black eyes flashing like those of a bird. Eventually, she produced a purse and popped it into the woman's hand. She opened the purse, and pulled out a ten pound note. She held the money out towards Ritchie.

'Now let me ask you a question. Have you seen anything unusual at this bus stop?'

5 The tenner

THE 971 from school strained up the hill. Instead of looking over Gloria's shoulder at the dials on the dashboard as usual, Ritchie focused his eyes firmly on the bus stop ahead. The crow was there, but there was no sign of anyone else. Woody wasn't around – that was good, because Ritchie had had enough rough stuff for one day.

The door sighed open and Gloria waved him goodbye. 'Bye, Ritchie,' she smiled. 'Make sure you be a good boy.'

Ritchie grinned nervously – he knew he hadn't been good that day.

At lunchtime, Connor Collins and his two mates, Psychic and Delaney – the Collins gang – had grabbed Ritchie outside the canteen. They'd pulled him up the bank, which was out of sight of the school. Delaney had stood on his hand while Psychic had kept watch, and Connor demanded the money he said Ritchie "owed" him.

Ritchie tried to say that he didn't have any money, but Psychic said he was lying. They went through his pockets and found the ten pound note. They said they'd see him again next week for the next "instalment".

Ritchie was angry with himself. The day before he'd told the Tall Woman everything she wanted to know, just to get the money to pay off Connor. But it hadn't worked. Connor wanted more, and now Ritchie felt bad about talking to the Tall Woman about what had been happening at the bus stop. He kept telling himself that there was no reason for this. Nobody had told him anything that was a secret; in fact, nobody had told him that anything was actually going on at all. He just had this feeling that maybe he shouldn't have told her what he knew just so that he could have some money for Collins.

Ritchie watched the bus drive away up the First Hill. After beating the hedge around the gate with a big stick to make sure the weirdo Woody wasn't around, he went back to his game inside the bus stop.

All the stones had been kicked and scuffed out of shape. Quietly he started to put Camp Bastion back together with its observation towers, machine gun nests and camouflaged armoured vehicles. Slowly he began to forget about Connor Collins, Delaney and Psychic and all the other things that had happened. In his pocket he had a letter for his dad from the head of year. The school wanted to see them both. He forgot about that.

Ritchie stopped playing when he noticed two dusty shoes standing next to some of the outlying Taliban positions. He looked up. The shoes led up to a pair of grimy pin-striped trousers, held around a fat stomach by a belt with the word 'King' written on it next to the face of Elvis Presley, with a check shirt above it. The familiar brown-eyed face of Kid Welly looked down at him.

'Mind if I intervene for an instant, boy?' said Kid.

Ritchie shook his head. 'No,' he said, then he remembered his message. 'I saw Doc Penfro here. He told me to tell you that he's good for whatever you see fit.'

'Did you tell him that I was here?' asked Kid.

'Of course I did,' replied Ritchie.

'Good boy. I'm surprised I haven't run into him yet,' said Kid. 'It's not a big town you've got here.'

'There's a ferry, a train, a supermarket … what more do you want?'

'I'm just saying it's not so big that a man as conspicuous as Doc could hole up in it without being noticed by a man as observant as me,' said Kid.

Ritchie stood up. 'There was a woman too, she got off the bus,' he said.

'So? A lot of women go around by bus. I'd say around half the people on buses are women, so what's so special about this one?'

'Tall, thin, wearing black,' said Ritchie. 'And she had a friend.'

'Again, Ritchie, I'm not following you – why is that unusual? There are tall thin women in this world and, I dare say, many of them have friends.'

'They asked me questions.'

'Was this friend kind of short, about seventeen years old with a square jaw, jet black hair and mean-looking eyes?' asked Kid.

'Kind of,' said Ritchie. 'I'd say her eyes were probably mean.'

Ritchie shuffled awkwardly; he could tell Kid didn't like the newcomers.

'What's the matter, boy?' asked Kid.

'I told her you were here,' he said.

'Now why did you do a dumb think like that?' asked Kid.

'I didn't think it mattered,' said Ritchie.

'But now you think it does?' asked Kid.

'Yes,' replied Ritchie. 'She was very interested in the two of you. Do you know her?'

Kid Welly thought for a moment. 'Everybody knows her. You could say she's a kind of witch and the girl is kind of her apprentice. The girl looks mean because she's not very good – she's slow on the uptake, if you get my drift. She's not a natural – not like you,' said Kid. 'Do me a favour, boy.'

Ritchie nodded.

'Apart from me and Doc, don't talk to any more strangers.'

'You know there's a weirdo in the hedge?' asked Ritchie.

'As a matter of fact, I didn't,' said Kid. 'What's his name?'

'Woody.'

'Never heard of him,' said Kid. 'Don't talk to him either. When you see Doc, tell him I'll be waiting for him in town. Tell him we haven't got long.'

'Long for what?'

Kid moved closer to Ritchie. 'There's a crow perched on the roof of this bus stop. He's listening to everything we say. Just stop blabbing to everyone who gets off a bus and wise up. Tell Doc what I said and wait for instructions. We're going to need your assistance. If you've a mind to help, I'd be most grateful.'

'Me?' asked Ritchie. 'Why me?'

''Cos you're a One Off.'

With that, Kid strode out of the bus stop and back down towards the town. As he moved away, Annie Bike zoomed past him, pedalling as hard as she could. She swerved across the road, scratching to a halt outside the bus stop. She'd been playing netball. She wore her school blazer over her Goal Attack shirt, her shoes were stuffed into the bag slung over her back and her trainers were covered in mud.

'How weird is he?' she sighed. 'What you doing, Ritchie? We won, by the way, 10–4. Wanna know who scored the 10?'

Ritchie was pleased to see Annie. She was the only normal person he could talk to, and even though he'd just promised not to speak to strangers, he told Annie as much as he could because she wasn't a stranger to him. In fact, Ritchie knew that Annie thought that *he* was the stranger. He'd only been living in the cottage on her farm for a few months, whilst Annie had been in her farm all her life. Annie listened, smiling politely, thinking to herself that Ritchie was just playing one of his games. She liked calling in at the bus stop to see what names he'd given to the stones, to throw sticks at land-mines and to hear his stories about the pirate speed-boats that were waiting just around the headland to ambush the ferry. She didn't believe a word of what Ritchie said, but she thought he was funny.

'You're telling me that the crow is a kind of a spy?' she said, looking up at the bird on the roof.

'I don't know whose side he's on. All I know is that he can understand everything we're saying,' said Ritchie.

The crow turned its head.

'How can you tell?' asked Annie.

Ritchie looked slightly embarrassed, almost nervous. 'Well, that guy said so,' he said, pointing at the distant figure of Kid Welly striding down the hill.

'He's a Country and Western nutcase. He doesn't know anything,' said Annie.

'And …' Ritchie's voice trailed away, 'there's the sheep – the black sheep. He understands me.'

The field was still empty, but Annie knew the one he meant – they were her sheep. Ritchie seemed embarrassed; he wished he hadn't told Annie that he thought the animals could understand him.

'Shemi?' she asked.

'Who?' blinked Ritchie.

'Shemi. We named him because he stands out. A real stroppy ram,' explained Annie. 'He's my pet sheep. We don't normally keep black rams, but Shemi's different.'

'Yes, him,' admitted Ritchie.

'You talk to the sheep?' laughed Annie.

'Just Shemi; the rest are pretty dull,' said Ritchie.

Annie laughed. She ruffled Ritchie's hair. 'You're a mad boy. Come on, I'm taking you for a ride on my bike.'

Ritchie didn't really want to go on Annie's bike; it was too wobbly and she rode too fast. But she insisted it would be OK. She got him to sit on the seat and hold her waist as she stood on the pedals and steered them up the Winding Lane to the houses. Once they got going it was brilliant; Ritchie shouted out loud at the top of his voice.

The crow watched them. Hidden all around the stop, other eyes followed their zigzag route up the Winding Lane. Ritchie laughed out loud as Annie pretended to pedal as hard as she could. She could actually go a lot faster.

6 The Spannermen

AT FIVE minutes past eight in the morning Ritchie crossed the road to the bus stop, sucking his red sweet. The sky was dull, the clouds hung low over the cliffs, blocking out the vapour trails of the passenger planes above, and the distant sea spread out like a sheet of steel. Ritchie stuck his hand in his pocket and felt the note – the one from school he was supposed to have given to his dad. He cursed himself for forgetting. They'd probably give him another note, explaining how he had stopped taking notes home from school. He knew this could end up getting serious, because if you didn't give the notes to your parents you could get suspended.

Ritchie was lost in his thoughts as he made his way into the bus stop. He ignored the inquisitive crow and Shemi the sheep, who was hanging about by the gate, waiting nervously. He stepped straight into the bus stop and tripped over. Ritchie toppled forwards, uncertain of what had caught his feet. There was a slight groan. Ritchie stuck his hands out and caught himself on the bus timetable noticeboard. He regained his balance, turned and saw a terrible sight: Woody, the green man, lay on the ground, green blood oozing out of a gash in his head.

Ritchie jumped over to him and knelt down. 'Woody, are you OK?'

Woody groaned again. 'Blinkin' marvellous,' he moaned. 'Abso-blinkin'-lutely tick-a-dee-boo.'

Woody's head lolled back; he'd lost consciousness.

Ritchie didn't know what to do. The 971 bus to school was due to arrive in ten minutes. He couldn't just get on it and leave Woody. He thought quickly. What would his dad have done if he was still in the army? The answer was obvious – dig in, take cover and look after the injured man. So Ritchie dragged Woody by the shoulders out of the bus stop, towards the gate, where Shemi stood watching.

He pulled Woody down into the ditch by the hedge and propped him on the stone field boundary through which most of the vegetation was growing. Down here, Woody was out of sight. Then Ritchie grabbed some cover – twigs and branches – and spread them out above the ditch. He needed water. There was a dustbin near the bus stop; Ritchie looked inside and found an empty lemonade bottle. He pulled it out, climbed over the gate and ran down to the bottom of the field where there was a little stream. He came back with the water and splashed it on Woody's face, cleaning the cut on his head, then he poured some into his rubbery green mouth. Slowly Woody's eyes flickered back open – one black, one blue. The water seemed to be making him feel a bit better.

'Oh, my head,' groaned Woody.

'What happened?' asked Ritchie.

Woody thought for a moment, then, as he remembered, a look of fear crossed his face.

'Spannermen!' he said. 'Hundreds of them. They come marching through in the night. Woody sleeps. They find him. They catch him. They try to toast him on their metal melting fires. The Spannermen go to eat Woody like a chicken going round and round in a chip shop. Not wanting to eat *with* Woody, you understand, but to eat Woody!'

Ritchie listened with horror. Woody was a very ugly creature, but Ritchie didn't think he really deserved to be eaten. And anyway, he imagined he'd taste rotten; eating Woody would be like eating a green slimy frog.

'Who are the Spannermen?' asked Ritchie.

'An army on the march. They're also looking for the source as well as Woody. They can feel the power here too.'

'An army of what? Where are they?'

'All around and hidden,' said Woody, waving his arms, 'in their metal suits with their clanking swords.'

'What, like knights?' asked Ritchie. 'In suits of armour?'

'Spannermen!' shouted Woody, 'Always tightening, always fighting.'

Ritchie stood up. He could see the 971 on the road at the Second Hill. 'How did you escape?'

'I made myself small and grafted through the ground. The Spannermen are slow in their metal, but they cop Woody on the blinkin' head with a spiky stick. Later he falls over in Ritchie's house,' said Woody, pointing at the bus stop. 'Ritchie's made his house on a magic place – Ritchie's house has healing powers.'

Ritchie didn't have long; the bus was at the top of the First Hill. 'Take the water,' he said. 'If you need anything, ask the sheep.'

Shemi watched and rolled his letterbox eyes.

'Look after Woody,' shouted Ritchie to the black sheep as he scrambled out of the ditch and ran towards the bus stop. 'I'll be back after school.'

Ritchie just about made it to the stop in time to put his hand out for the bus. He'd never not waved for the bus. It was really unlucky not to wave. Gloria was driving and she opened the doors.

'Morning, Ritchie,' she said in her sing-song voice. 'You OK, boy? You look like you've seen a ghost.'

Ritchie grinned and took a seat. He didn't sit in his normal place behind the driver; he went further down the bus and sat on the side next to the bus stop, so he could see Shemi. He was relieved to see that the camouflage had worked. There was no sign of Woody.

7 The big meeting

RITCHIE DIDN'T want to go home after school. The head of year had rung his dad and they'd arranged a meeting. Jamie didn't have any idea why they wanted to see him because Ritchie still had the note from school in his pocket. It had been a day of disasters in school, but Ritchie did manage to get a packet of crisps and a bottle of coke, and keep away from the Collins gang.

Ritchie stepped off the 971 at ten past four. He waited for it to disappear before hurrying to the spot where he'd left Woody. He wanted to give him the supplies, to help him feel better. But when he arrived at the ditch there was no sign of Woody, and Shemi and the other sheep had wandered off to a distant part of the field. Ritchie decided to leave the supplies in the ditch. He reasoned that there was a good chance Woody was around, hiding deep in some hedge, and that he could probably see him. He could come for the supplies later.

Ritchie returned from the ditch and sat in the bus stop. He didn't know what to do. He didn't feel like playing as there was too much going on at the bus stop and in his head. He knew that his dad would be really mad with him because of the phone call. He didn't want to go home and have to answer Jamie's questions, but he didn't really want to stay at the bus stop either. It was getting kind of scary there too.

A taxi pulled up by the stop and two familiar men climbed out. It was Doc Penfro and Kid Welly. Kid gave the driver a twenty pound note and told him to keep the change. They waved at Ritchie and strolled over, swaggering in their cowboy hats. Ritchie felt almost relieved to see them. The crow, who was perched on a telegraph pole nearby, was beginning to get to him. The bird was like a security camera, thought Ritchie, always watching, reporting back to someone or something with all the news from the bus stop.

'Well, how-dee, Little Richard?' said Doc, as he

swaggered into the bus stop, stooping slightly to stop the tip of his hat touching the roof.

Kid Welly, still wearing his Elvis belt pulled tight around his big belly, strode into the bus stop too. 'We found each other,' he said.

Ritchie thought that this was obvious.

'It's been a long time,' Doc continued. 'Kid and I were once famous in these parts. We were a great team.'

'It's how we got our names,' said Kid. 'The Doc and the Kid. He comes from Pembroke Dock, you see, and I'm from Kidwelly.'

Ritchie nodded. He was thinking about his dad. He was going to go absolutely mad.

'And now we're riding together again,' said Doc, slapping Kid on the back.

'Outlaws in a world full of in-laws,' added Kid.

Ritchie looked at the two of them. They didn't look very scary; they didn't look like real outlaws at all.

'So after we met up, down in the town, we thought we'd better come and see you, Little Ritchie. After all, you're the man who brought us together.'

'I didn't bring you together,' said Ritchie. 'I just took a couple of messages.'

'Ritchie, you did enough. You told us the truth and we appreciate that,' said Kid.

Ritchie thought about his dad – he wished he'd told him the truth.

'So now it's time to level with you,' said Doc. 'You wanna ride with us?'

'We ain't got horses, so we use the word loosely,' explained Kid. 'You wanna join us?'

Ritchie didn't want to be in Doc and Kid's gang. He didn't like gangs. He thought there was a strong chance they'd give him a stupid check shirt and a sheriff's badge to wear, so he shook his head.

'I like that,' said Doc. 'The boy rides alone; that's why he's a One Off.'

'Will somebody please tell me what a One Off is,' asked Ritchie.

'We'll level with you, Ritchie. We'll tell you the truth, but we need your help – we need you to ride with us,' said Doc.

'Or at least walk,' added Kid.

'OK,' sighed Ritchie. 'I'll ride with you.'

'I knew you'd see sense,' said Kid, grinning. 'Acquaint him, Doc.'

Kid's eyebrows came together. He looked serious as Doc drew himself to his full height and began to speak. 'A One Off happens very occasionally – a human being who has the ability to see into other worlds, worlds that exist in the same space as the human dimension,' said Doc, clearing his throat and spitting on the floor.

'A One Off can sense things – feelings, vibes, powers,' said Kid.

'A One Off can see stuff – ancient things, strange creatures, things that all the other humans would describe as "made up",' explained Doc.

'They call it superstition, they call them ghosts, werewolves, zombies, vampires – but actually these are just words used by people who are not One Offs, who can't see anything. You have seen a Green Man, haven't you?'

Ritchie nodded his head, almost feeling guilty.

'You can understand animals and they get you,' said Kid.

'Yeah, kind of,' said Ritchie.

'And you met a sorceress,' said Doc. 'Several, actually. They're all coming here. To this bus stop.'

Ritchie shook his head. He hadn't met any sorceresses.

'Oh come on – she came on the bus, she gave you money, she asked you about us,' said Doc.

'And what are you? asked Ritchie. 'A couple of Country and Western singers.' He moved away from Doc and Kid.

'We do sing a little Country, but that's just our cover,' said Doc. 'We look like a couple of folk artists, but actually … we're different too. I suppose we're sorcerers too. You understand?'

Ritchie shook his head.

'What do you know about Spannermen?' asked Doc.

'They're like knights in armour. There's an army of them camped around here,' said Ritchie.

'You seen 'em?'

Ritchie shook his head again.

'Well they are here. This place is filling up with creatures from the old underworld. Every day, new ones arrive. Have you stopped to ask yourself why?' said Doc.

This time Ritchie nodded. He didn't like the way his bus stop had changed.

'They're scared,' said Kid. 'We're all scared.'

'Why?' asked Ritchie.

'You got a minute or two?' said Kid.

Ritchie had more than a minute or two – he didn't want to go home at all.

'Yes,' replied Ritchie.

'OK,' said Kid, 'sit down.'

They all sat down on the ground in the bus stop. Kid Welly picked up a few of the stones and pebbles Ritchie used to play with.

'You mind if I use your items?' asked Kid.

'No,' said Ritchie.

'A One Off has the imagination to see things in other things; it's how we found you. You make these stones whatever you want them to be,' explained Doc. 'Isn't that just what a sorcerer does? You've got a sorcerer's imagination.' Doc rolled the stone around between his fingers. 'One minute it's a tank, the next it's a ship, then it's a jet – always transforming.'

Ritchie nodded slowly.

'OK,' said Ritchie. 'Tell me what's going on.'

Kid ran his hand over the tarmac until he found what he wanted. He held up a tiny white pebble. 'You see this?'

Ritchie nodded.

'This is evil.' Kid placed the stone carefully on the ground. 'Now I'm going to tell you about the end of the world.'

8 The Blue Stone

KID WELLY cast his eyes from the sea to the land and focused on the Old Mountains, misty and sandy in the evening light. His brown eyes gleamed as he surveyed the hills.

'Do you know what an "intersection" is?' he asked.

Ritchie shook his head.

'It's the point where two lines cross. You've found one. You come to it all the time. You may not understand it yourself yet, but you feel it. That's 'cos you're special. This bus stop is on the intersection of two ancient lines – it's part of a web that links this place to Stonehenge, to the Pyramids of Egypt and to the underworld.'

Ritchie thought about the bus stop. He got the idea. The buses followed one line, the planes flying overhead to and from America followed another. His bus stop was the point where they met. It was part of the reason why he liked it there.

'I get "intersections",' said Ritchie.

'A long time ago – I'm talking ages, right back in time, before people had really taken over the world – things were different,' Kid continued.

'How d'you mean?' asked Ritchie.

Kid sighed. 'I can't tell you this story but if you ask questions I'll lose my way. You have to listen,' he said.

'But I want to know what you mean. When was this? How were things different? Are we in the time of knights in armour?' asked Ritchie.

'Before that,' said Kid, 'before the people learned to make iron, before the bronze makers, at the time when a stone was "the best a man could get". Imagine trying to shave with a stone.'

Ritchie couldn't do this. Doc could, and he stroked his chin.

'Couldn't be done,' said Kid, 'so these stone people were beardy – beardy people who used stones to cut stuff.'

'Stone-age people,' said Ritchie.

'You've got it, boy. Now, there weren't so many

of these stone-age people and, because they only had stones to work with, they weren't so good at chopping trees down, building roads and making ships. They got about, but slowly, and they lived with the animals. In fact, this was such a long time ago that they were almost animals. They were animals who used stones. *We* are animals who use ...'

Kid looked around for inspiration.

'... who use buses,' added Ritchie.

'Got it in one,' said Kid. 'We like to think we're quite separate from nature. But we're not – we're just animals who use buses. They were close to nature in them days. They knew the way of the world better,' said Doc. 'Because of that, *they* knew things *we*'ve forgotten. They could talk to animals, or at least understand them, and they understood the power of these things – like you.'

Kid picked up some more of Ritchie's pebbles and placed them in a curling line around the first stone, making a swirl shape, the same shape that Ritchie found them in a few days earlier. He gasped.

'Stones,' said Kid. 'The power is in the stones. You know that.'

'What power?' asked Ritchie.

'They stood stones up, they moved them around, they lined them up with the big stones in the sky, like the moon, and by doing this they contacted the power of nature. Their biggest stones were at Stonehenge – they're still there. And the stones they used to build the circles at Stonehenge were very powerful indeed and came from around here. They were the Blue Stones. It was said that if you could touch a Blue Stone, you'd be cured of whatever was wrong with you. The Blue Stones were powerful; more powerful than anything you could dream of.'

'I still don't see what that's got to do with us, here now,' said Ritchie.

Kid continued to lay his pebbles on the ground until he'd finished the spiral pattern. 'The tribes knew about the power in the stones, but they only had a few "One Offs" – people who could *really* sense what was happening. These stones were the ones that connected people to the power of nature. They started taking the stones from here and standing them up in other places. The folks around here didn't like people taking the stones. They'd pull them off the sacred hillsides and spirit them away. So one particular One Off,

60

who was watching this happen, said to his mates – "we'll keep one back – just in case".'

Ritchie nodded.

'You imagine the scene – beardy stone-age people from all over the country crawling around these hills. There are people who are pretending to be One Offs, and there are real One Offs. There are witches and wizards, all kinds of cranks and fairy-story makers, all of them trying to get hold of those big blue stones. Some people want to move the stones from the mountains to the plains, and one kid and a few of his mates from around these parts have got this idea – they want to steal a magic stone and hide it, so that it stays put, where it should be. And that's what they do. They keep one back – the most powerful one they could find – just in case.'

'OK ...' said Ritchie, 'so thousands of years ago a guy from around here stole a magic stone. So what?'

'He didn't steal it,' said Doc. 'He kept it back. It's here somewhere.'

'It got lost,' added Kid. 'Or at least, when they invented bronze, then iron, wars happened, gods changed, everything changed. They forgot the magic in the stone and so it kinda fizzled out.

Well, it didn't disappear; it stayed where it was. What really happened was that people couldn't remember where it was or even how to see it.'

'They lost it,' added Doc.

'So, why is this important?' asked Ritchie, who was beginning to think that the story was very unlikely to be true.

'Protection,' said Kid.

'Defence,' said Doc.

'Keeping everything together,' said Kid.

'I don't understand,' said Ritchie. 'If the stone's so powerful, isn't it dangerous?'

Kid laughed. 'You could say, if it fell into the wrong hands. But nobody can find the stone – it could be anywhere. It's been lost for five thousand years. It was stolen by a few blokes from this village – maybe not all that different from us.'

'Apart from the beards,' noted Ritchie.

'The danger is the part I'm going to tell you now – the part that is stirring up all the old sorcerers and ghosts who have been hanging about, watching the world change, the part that has put the Spannermen on the march.' Kid leant forward, half whispering: 'They are all scared. They realise that the power in the stone is their last line of defence, and without the stone they will be wiped out forever. And they are scared in case the King finds it first.'

'Who is the King?' asked Ritchie, whose head was beginning to hurt with all the sorcery stuff.

Doc looked wide-eyed at Ritchie – he couldn't believe it was possible for someone not to have heard of the King.

'They say he rides a black horse across the night sky so he cannot be seen. They say he takes the form of a crow, or sometimes a beetle,' said Kid.

'He makes volcanoes explode and he creates hurricanes and water spouts; he starts wars and he puts the destruction into nature, he … he wants to grind everything into nothing,' said Doc.

'It's a little hard to explain who he is,' said Kid. 'I can tell you what he isn't – he's not like an ordinary man or a woman, he's not even like an ordinary being from the underworld, he's not even like an ordinary god,' said Kid. 'He wants to destroy us all. To do that, he must find the missing blue stone. He's on his way to your little intersection because he's heard about the One Off who stole it from him in the first place. We've got to beat him to it.'

'We've gotta look after ourselves,' added Doc.

Ritchie looked doubtful.

'Are you telling me that there's a magic stone around here – and that it's the only thing stopping the King – whoever he is – from destroying the world?'

'Clever boy. You put it very concisely. You're a One Off and no mistake,' said Doc.

'He's got all the others. It's the last lost stone,' said Kid.

Kid pointed to the crow, pecking the ground outside the bus stop. 'He's following you.'

Ritchie stared at Kid. He shook his head as if he was shaking out all of Kid's words. 'What a load of rubbish. That crow has nothing to do with the end of the world. Nor do I.'

'I'm telling you boy, you're a One Off. You've got to help us find that stone before the King takes it and destroys the lot of us,' said Kid.

'I'm *not* a One Off and I haven't got a clue what you're talking about. How can you possibly know that this is true?'

'We don't,' admitted Doc, 'but there are stories.'

'That's exactly what this is,' said Ritchie. 'A story. You're a couple of crappy Country and Western con artists. How can you possibly know anything about what happened all that time ago?'

'We keep our eyes and ears open,' replied Kid.

'We've been around since the dawn of time,' said Doc. 'And so have you. You took the stone in the first place.'

Ritchie looked at the two men, ridiculous in their broad brimmed hats.

'I'm *not* a One Off and there *is* no King,' shouted Ritchie.

The bristles on Kid's chin prickled with rage and his enormous eyebrows knitted together across his forehead. Ritchie sprang to his feet and ran from the bus stop. As he emerged, a red car appeared at the end of the Winding Lane leading to his house. It was Jamie; he looked angry too. He sped across the road and pulled up with a screech by the bus stop. Rock 'n' Roll music spread out across the road.

Doc and Kid spilled out of the bus stop. They hadn't seen Ritchie's dad. They both ran after Ritchie who sprinted straight towards Jamie's car. As Jamie opened his door to get out Ritchie threw himself into his dad's arms and hugged him. Even Jamie was surprised at this. He couldn't think of a time when Ritchie had ever hugged him.

'Dad!' shouted Ritchie.

Jamie turned the music down. 'Don't you "Dad" me,' he snarled.

Kid and Doc stopped running and jogged to a halt. They pretended they were chasing a bus.

'Missed it,' said Doc loudly so that Jamie could hear him. 'That pesky bus! We were just a few seconds late.'

'Darn it!' added Kid.

They turned to Ritchie and Jamie.

'Good to meet you, boy, and thanks for your help with the bus,' said Kid.

'Be seeing you, sir. That's a fine boy you've got there,' said Doc, tipping his hat towards Jamie.

Jamie smiled suspiciously at the two cowboys as they walked quickly down the road towards the town.

'Friends of yours?' asked Jamie.

'Kind of,' said Ritchie. 'They … errr … missed their bus.'

'You know what?' said Jamie. 'I don't care.'

Ritchie remembered the note from school.

'You've been hanging around down here because you're avoiding me. Well, you've got to come home some time or other, and now's as good as any. We're going back.'

'But Dad!' moaned Ritchie.

'The school phoned me today. They want to talk to me about putting you in the special unit. They tried not to make it sound too bad, but between you and me, it's simple. You're a dead loss. You read like a five year old, you write like a baby, you can't play football and you don't talk to anyone. They think you're a loser, Ritchie,' shouted Jamie.

Ritchie hung his head as his dad went on: 'I think you're a loser. You don't work, you don't have friends, you just mess about on your own down here.'

'What do *you* do?' whispered Ritchie.

Unfortunately Jamie heard. 'What did you say?' he said, anger flashing in his eyes.

'You do just the same as me,' blurted Ritchie. 'But instead of coming down here you just stay at home, drink cans and watch telly. You don't know anybody, you don't work, you don't do anything,'

'It's true I don't do anything. I stay at home because I can't get out. I'm a bloody cripple. I don't talk to people because they don't like me being around. I've got more metal in my legs than a pair of scaffolding poles. I trod on a bomb in Afghanistan. Something made me like this. I didn't look around one day thinking, "Hmmm, what shall I do today? I know – I'll find a little land-mine and see if that hurts." I was unlucky, and now I'm paying the price. You, on the other hand, are just plain lazy and stupid. Nobody blew you up, Ritchie. You just expect it all on a plate. Get in the car.'

Ritchie climbed into the car.

9 Shemi

THE EVENING up in Ritchie's little cottage had gone very badly. Jamie was angry and kept going on about his bad luck. He threw a book across the little living room at Ritchie.

'Read,' he shouted. Ritchie opened the book and tried to, but it was one of his dad's books and the words were close together. 'You can read something I like – something grown up. No wonder you can't read that school stuff – it's chuffing dull.'

'You don't know what it's like,' said Ritchie. 'I can see the words, but not the letters – it's weird.'

Ritchie tried to read.

'My wife runs off with my best mate, I get blown up, I lose a leg. "Unlucky" you might say, "but never mind, things might get better." Then what? I tell you what, Ritchie – being stuck up here

69

in this chuffing farmhouse with you puts the tin lid on it. You're a waste of space.'

Jamie leapt from his chair and snatched the book from his son. He looked at the word Ritchie was trying to read.

'Detachment,' he shouted 'It says: "The chuffing detachment beat a hasty retreat to the high ground where they dug in and bivouacked for the night".'

Ritchie started to cry.

Jamie opened a can of beer. 'Go to bed,' he snapped.

Ritchie didn't want to.

'GO!' his dad shouted.

Ritchie went.

Ritchie couldn't sleep. Whenever he dosed off he kept having weird nightmares about ghostly armies of Spannermen trying to cut him up. Later that night he listened as Jamie stumbled around on the landing before finding his room and going to bed. He heard his dad's bedroom door close.

'Are you lonesome tonight? ...'

Ritchie waited for his dad to sing himself to sleep, then slowly sneaked out of his room, slipped down the little wooden staircase and into the hall with the stone floor. There, in a big green kit-bag, was his dad's torch. He took the torch and tiptoed through the kitchen and out into the starless night. The torch, like all of his dad's kit, was big and powerful. It lit up the Winding Lane down to the main road with silver light. Ritchie shone it on the bus stop. The crow, invisible in the black night, blinked at him from its seemingly permanent perch on the roof. Ritchie trotted over the road and straight to the gate where he'd left the crisps for Woody. He carried with him a plastic bag with some bread in it, more water and some sticking plasters.

Ritchie wasn't surprised to find Woody had returned, but he still jumped when the torchlight picked him out.

'It's OK, it's only me,' whispered Ritchie, as he shone the light into his own face so that Woody could see.

'Ritchie, what are you doing here in this ditch?' asked Woody, smiling.

Ritchie explained that he couldn't sleep; he was worried about all sorts of stuff. Ritchie felt really bad about Jamie, even though in the end Jamie had said that he didn't mean most of the stuff he said. Ritchie was worried about Woody too; that's why he'd brought the extra supplies.

Woody ate the bread and drank the water. Ritchie stuck two sticking plasters onto the cut on Woody's head. The plasters looked strange on his rubbery green skin.

'It's this place,' said Woody. 'There's something special about it.'

'The bus stop?' asked Ritchie.

'Yes, here is where it comes from – the power,' said Woody. 'Don't know why, don't know how.'

'It's an intersection,' said Ritchie. Even in the middle of the night he preferred the bus stop to home.

Ritchie sat down next to Woody and asked him more questions. Woody confessed that he had heard about the Blue Stone and its magical powers, and that he wanted it for himself, for protection.

'The only problem is,' said Woody, 'every other blinkin' creature wants it too.'

'Have you ever heard of the King?' asked Ritchie.

Woody shook his head, cramming more bread into his mouth. 'Those cowboys made that up to give you the heebie-jeebies,' he said. 'The King is a load of blinkin' eyewash. The one that they really want is you.'

'Why?' asked Ritchie.

'Because you're a One Off. A One Off doesn't go away. They can't go away. You are the one who nicked the blinkin' stone in the first place. You can take them to the stone,' shouted Woody, 'but you will take Woody instead.'

Ritchie shook his head; he didn't know anything about magical stones.

There was a sharp crack a little way off, somewhere in the night. Woody dived down into the ditch, pulling Ritchie with him and smothering the torchlight.

'Shut your blinkin' cake hole and watch,' hissed Woody, clamping his hand over Ritchie's mouth. 'It's the Spannermen, all tight in their metal.'

Ritchie flicked the torch off. They lay in silence. It wasn't the Spannermen; it was Annie Bike and her dad. They were walking around the field, wrapped up in big coats, also carrying torches. As they passed the gate, Ritchie heard them talking. They were speaking in Welsh. Their voices sounded serious. They weren't laughing – they were looking. Annie's dad carried a shotgun under his arm, Annie held the light. As they moved off Ritchie stared after them, wide-eyed. He turned to Woody. Woody – all rubbery and green – blinked at him slowly. Ritchie didn't understand. The ancient words reverberated

73

around his head. He knew he couldn't understand Welsh. He'd only been with Jamie in the cottage for six months; long enough to pick up a few words, but not enough to really get it. But somehow Ritchie knew exactly what Annie and her dad were talking about. Shemi, Annie's pet, had been stolen and her dad was going to give whoever did it both barrels.

Ritchie whispered to Woody, unsure how he'd understood what he heard.

'See,' said Woody triumphantly, 'Ritchie's a One Off. You understand all sorts of stuff. What's going on?'

'Woody, that's not The Spannermen,' said Ritchie. 'It's my friend Annie. Shemi's been taken by sheep rustlers.'

Woody looked blankly at Ritchie, it seemed he had no idea what Ritchie was on about, whatever language he spoke.

'Shemi the sheep,' said Ritchie. 'The one who looked after you this morning.'

'Oh him,' said Woody. 'Sheep don't mean diddly-squat to Woody.'

'Now who do you think would do sheep rustling around here?' asked Ritchie.

Woody thought for a moment, his brow

furrowed, causing his sticking plasters to move around on his head.

'How should I know?' said Woody.

'Isn't rustling something cowboys do?' asked Ritchie. 'But what would Doc and Kid want with a sheep like Shemi?'

'Mint sauce and gravy?' suggested Woody. 'Maybe a few potatoes and some baby spinach?'

Ritchie sighed and looked into Woody's multi-coloured eyes. 'I don't know what kind of creature from the underworld you are, Woody, but can I ask you a question?'

'Fire-a-blinkin'-way,' said Woody.

'Do you have any special powers? You know, like you can see clearly what's going on, you understand everything because you've been alive for thousands of years – maybe you were here when they found the Blue Stone in the first place.'

'Oh yes. Woody was here then, with all the beardy stony people,' said Woody.

'So where's the stone? What did they do with it? asked Ritchie.

'Woody doesn't remember stuff like that,' said Woody, 'Woody doesn't remember blinkin' diddly-squat. Woody got different special powers.'

'Go on,' sighed Ritchie, 'what is it that makes you special?'

'Digging,' said Woody. 'Woody can dig like a blinkin' JCB.'

Ritchie sighed. It was so typical – the only weird creature that seemed prepared to tell him the truth couldn't remember it!

'Oh well,' said Ritchie, 'people under-rate digging. I say, "If you can dig – you can groove".'

'Exactly,' said Woody. 'If you can dig, you can groove".'

Woody did a little dance. Ritchie laughed.

'Look,' said Ritchie, 'can you do some digging?'

Woody laughed: 'Can a fish swim?'

'See if you can find Shemi, then. If Doc and Kid have taken him, he can't be far away.'

Woody thought for a moment. 'Blinkin' things to do. OK. For Ritchie, I'll find Shemi.'

With that, Woody scuttled off into the hedge. Ritchie walked back to the bus stop. He shone his big torch around, as if looking for clues – clues as to what was really going on. He flicked the beam around the bus stop. Nothing had changed; even the crow was still there. Ritchie felt angry; tears filled his eyes. He didn't know why. He thought about his dad at home and how sorry he felt that everything was rubbish. And then he considered himself and how angry he was that he was making everything rubbish. He was the one who couldn't make friends, who couldn't play sport and who couldn't read.

Ritchie shone the torch on the timetable. He looked at the lists of numbers and words, and then he noticed something. Someone had taken a thick pen and written graffiti all over it. Ritchie put his finger on the first word and read it slowly: 'Do', then he did the next one, and the next until he'd read them all. He said them out loud very slowly:

Do as we say or the sheep gets it.
Yours respectfully,
Doc and The Kid.

Ritchie looked around in horror. The road disappeared into a sea of shadows. Doc Penfro and Kid Welly couldn't be trusted. They wanted the stone for themselves. Ritchie wasn't going to fall for any more of their tricks.

10 Driving

RITCHIE AND his dad drove past the bus stop the following morning. Ritchie sucked on his red sweet and studied the stop. There was the crow, the empty field and an old lady sitting there. She wore a woolly brown coat and a woolly brown hat.

'Who's she?' asked Ritchie's dad as they drove along.

'I dunno her name,' said Ritchie. 'I've met her before. She's nice. She'll be there for ages if she's waiting for the 479 to Cardigan.'

Jamie laughed. 'If you spent half as much time studying books as you do bus timetables, they'd be sending you to university. She must be hot in all that woollen stuff.

'She's the Woolly Woman,' said Ritchie.

Jamie grinned as he drove. 'Nice one.'

Ritchie nodded. His dad seemed in a better mood. It was as if everything was better.

'Don't worry,' said Jamie. 'I'll tell them to get off your case – you can't help it.'

Ritchie didn't find his dad's attitude so reassuring. Somehow the fact that he didn't expect him to do very well made Ritchie feel that even his dad really did think he was a loser.

'You're a good boy,' said Jamie. 'You help me, and it's a shame you don't get any marks for doing that. I'm the biggest pain in the backside of the lot.'

Ritchie wasn't listening, though. As the bus stop disappeared behind them his eyes stayed fixed on the old lady. She was beckoning for him to join her.

'Dad?' asked Ritchie.

'What?' said Jamie.

'That land-mine.'

'My land-mine?'

'Yeah – do you think it was just bad luck, or did something make it happen?'

Jamie fell silent. 'I dunno.' He grinned sadly. 'Perhaps it had my name on it.'

When they arrived in school Ritchie went straight to find Annie. He asked her about Shemi. She was surprised Ritchie knew her sheep had been stolen, so she asked him how he found out. Ritchie told Annie he'd heard the search party the night before, and said that he'd help her find Shemi. He told her not to worry. Annie looked worried.

The rest of the day went badly. Miss Croons, the head of Special Needs, had explained to Jamie how worried about Ritchie she was. The fact that he couldn't write very well was stopping Ritchie from learning in all his subjects; the fact that he didn't read the books she gave Ritchie to help him wasn't helping either. Miss Croons also said that Ritchie had "social issues" with the other children in his classes. Ritchie knew what this meant – nobody liked him. Ritchie didn't mention the fact that it was worse than that. He didn't mention the fact that Connor Collins and his gang were after more money. Miss Croons then asked Jamie if everything was all right at home. She asked how he was coping, because she knew about his legs, the fact that he'd had to get his car fixed so he could drive it with just his hands, the fact that he didn't have a job. This really got Jamie angry. He shouted at her when she said she could get a social worker to come around and help out.

'We're fine,' shouted Jamie.

'That's the point,' said Miss Croons. 'You think you're fine, but you're not. Ritchie's not achieving. *You're* not achieving.'

But Jamie wasn't talking about Ritchie any more. He was really off on one. He shouted at Miss Croons for sitting around in a soft job whilst people like him went off in the army and risked their lives so that she could wander around passing judgement on people. Jamie told Miss Croons that he was a soldier and he didn't take orders from social workers. Ritchie couldn't help smiling at this. Miss Croons didn't know what to say. She stayed calm, though. She kept saying that she was only thinking of Ritchie.

Ritchie just sat there and listened. Neither of them asked him what he thought. He kind of switched off during the argument. He thought about the bus stop, about Woody searching for Shemi. And he wondered about Doc Penfro and Kid Welly's story. Was everything bad happening because the King was coming? Could they be right? Could the world really be about to end? Was it all down to a search for the last magic stone that could protect them against the King? Was he a One Off? Did *he* really steal the stone in the first place? How come he couldn't speak Welsh, Sheep or Crow, but he understood all three? Were his dad and Miss Croons screaming their heads off because the world was actually on the point of falling apart? Was finding the Blue Stone the only way to sort things out – something Ritchie had no idea how to do?

In the end Jamie stopped shouting. He said there was no point in talking any more. He said he'd make sure Ritchie read his books and, as he left, he said that the fact that they couldn't teach Ritchie to read better was more a reflection of the fact that they couldn't do their jobs than the fact that Ritchie couldn't read so well.

'My Ritchie's a really smart kid,' said Jamie, shoving his khaki jacket on and moving to the door. 'He's just a bit different to you lot. He's a bit of a one off.'

When Ritchie heard his dad use these words he stopped daydreaming. His eyes popped wide open. Perhaps he really was a One Off. Perhaps he really wasn't all that dumb after all.

Jamie stormed home, leaving Ritchie to get on with his lessons. Ritchie felt different. He couldn't say exactly why, because nothing good had actually happened, but he felt better. In fact, he thought, although things had just got worse, he felt better.

11 The King

RITCHIE SAT on the bus behind Gloria, watching the speedometer, wondering whether he really was a One Off.

As the bus approached the stop Ritchie was surprised to see the Woolly Woman still waiting. He knew that seven buses had passed her by that day.

'Bye, Ritchie. See you tomorrow,' shouted Gloria, tooting her horn.

He hopped off the bus and waved as he watched it go. Then he turned to the Woolly Woman. 'What do you want? Are you really waiting for the 479 or do you want to speak to me?' he asked.

The lady looked at the ground. The swirl of stones left by Kid the day before was still there. 'Did you make this?

'No,' replied Ritchie, 'but I know what it means.'

'Tell me,' she said.

Ritchie pointed to the white pebble in the middle of the swirl. 'That's the King,' he said, 'and all these little pebbles are everything else. And what's happening is that the King is sucking them in one by one and destroying everything. He's coming for the Blue Stone and when he finds it – pop! – goodbye to everything. It's been on the cards for thousands of years.'

The old lady nodded. 'You worked that out for yourself?' she asked.

'Kind of,' said Ritchie.

'There's another way of looking at it,' she said, picking up the little white stone in the middle and handing it to Ritchie. 'That's the Blue Stone, and everything stays in place because it's safe,' she said with a smile. 'Tell me, Ritchie, where do you think the Blue Stone is?'

'I dunno,' shrugged Ritchie. 'It could be anywhere – there's millions of stones around here.'

'But you're special – you can sense things, you can feel the power of the stone because you're special. You remember, don't you?'

'I've got special needs, you mean,' laughed

Ritchie. 'If I was smart I wouldn't have to read these stupid big print books for infant school kids.'

'You can read all right,' said the Woolly Woman. 'You just do it in a different way. You know exactly what's going on just by feeling it.'

Ritchie looked at the old woman. He couldn't quite make out her face under that big woolly hat.

'Don't trust the cowboys. They want the stone for themselves,' said the woman.

'What about Woody?' asked Ritchie.

'We all want to find the stone, but the King is the most dangerous because if he gets it things will get very bad indeed. Everything will stop. Keep that little pebble, Ritchie – my powers aren't as strong as they used to be. But if you're in trouble, throw it and see what happens. It might help,' said the Woolly Woman.

'Who are you?' asked Ritchie.

'I'm just an old woman,' said the Woolly Woman.

'How old?' asked Ritchie.

'Good question. I'm older than you can possibly imagine. Actually, I'm only just a little older than you. I'm what they used to call a goddess. When I was young people used to worship me. Now they've given me a bus pass. I'm an old woolly woman,' she sighed. 'I just don't want to see everything turn to dust – not after all this time.'

The shining blue 479 was pulling up the hill. Ritchie could see it slowing down as the old lady put her hand out. 'You won't see me again,' said the Woolly Woman. 'I'm too weak to take on all the spirits around here, but Ritchie, you're strong, you're a One Off – you can do it.'

'Do what?' asked Ritchie as she stepped onto the bus.

'Find the stone and stop the King,' she said with a smile. 'That's my bus.'

Mr Dickinson was driving the bus; he smiled and waved at Ritchie. 'Hiya Ritchie,' he shouted as he checked the old lady's bus pass. Then he drove off.

Ritchie felt the tiny stone in his hand. He felt like throwing it just to see what would happen. But he didn't. Instead he ran to the ditch by the gate.

'Woody!' he shouted at the top of his voice.

There was a shimmer in the hedge right down on the other side of the field. It was like dry sand blowing across a beach. It zoomed towards Ritchie, up the field, then it turned the corner and sped towards the gate. Suddenly, breathless, Woody tumbled out of the ground.

'Blinkin' keep it down,' hissed Woody.

'You found Shemi?' asked Ritchie.

'Woody found Shemi, but it's not a good blinkin' place to be,' said Woody. 'Got any supplies?'

Ritchie had picked up a pasta pot from the canteen in school, and he handed it to Woody.

'Shemi's in the town, tied up in a dark box,' said Woody as he chewed the top off the pasta pot. 'Them cowboys got him. They say they will only let him go when he tells them where the stone is. They say they're gonna use him to get you. They say that if you don't help them, Shemi ends up in the kebab shop.'

'Right,' said Ritchie, 'we need to rescue him.'

'Woody likes kebabs,' said Woody.

'We can't eat him; he's our mate,' said Ritchie.

'The Spannermen want to eat Woody,' said Woody.

'I don't know about these Spannermen – are you sure you're not just imagining things?'

Woody looked hurt. He jumped up and down with rage and excitement. 'They're blinkin' all over, they're like ants crawling all over the apple core.'

'Well, I haven't seen any of them,' said Ritchie.

'We've got to rescue Shemi, and then, perhaps we should find the Blue Stone.'

'Blinkin' unbelievable,' said Woody. 'Now Ritchie's talking. How we gonna do it?'

'I dunno, Let me think. I'll have to go home first and practise reading. I'll be back,' said Woody.

'Ritchie can read?' asked Woody.

'… Yeah,' said Ritchie.

'Blinkin' clever stuff,' said Woody, impressed.

'Meet me here, later,' said Ritchie.

'Ritchie's got a plan?' asked Woody.

'… Yeah,' replied Ritchie, which wasn't exactly true, but he knew he had to go home and practise reading. Ritchie would do anything to stop his dad from thinking he was a dead loss.

12 Home

THAT EVENING, Ritchie sat at the table and read his book from school. It was called *The Runaway*. It was all about a boy who ran away from home. Ritchie didn't think very much of it – and it took him ages to put all the letters in the words together. He did three pages. He could tell Jamie was pleased with him.

Then he watched some TV with Jamie before going to bed. Instead of going to sleep, he waited. To pass the time he read the bus timetables. Ritchie found the bus timetables much easier to read than books. Perhaps it was because they were full of lists, not sentences, and they were written up and down, instead of across. With the bus timetables Ritchie could follow the routes, allocate buses to drivers and imagine all the places they would go to.

That's why he'd stuck timetables all over the walls of his bedroom. Not just his bus, or Williams Brothers, or even Wales. Ritchie could work a journey from Haverfordwest to Istanbul just by looking at the lists on his bedroom wall.

Eventually, at about midnight, he heard Jamie climbing up the stairs. He'd drunk too many cans, he was wobbly and had to use banisters and walls to stop him toppling off his legs. Ritchie heard him muttering to himself: 'Chuffing rockabilly legs!' as he sang his favourite Elvis song: 'Are you lonesome tonight?'

Ten minutes later, Ritchie slipped downstairs. Quietly, he rummaged through his dad's kit which he kept in the cupboard in the hall. There were all sorts of useful things in there, mostly from the army – bits of old camouflage netting, a big torch, webbing and a balaclava. Ritchie pulled the balaclava over his head, taking the torch and the camouflage netting. He knew Woody wouldn't be spotted – he was green already – but Ritchie might stick out in the night without camouflage.

Ritchie slipped out of the house and ran down the Winding Lane; he crossed the deserted road and arrived at the empty, eerie bus stop. The night was black and cold.

'Woody,' hissed Ritchie.

Woody was sleeping in his dugout. He opened his eyes. 'Blinkin' what's going on?' he exclaimed.

Ritchie told him that they were on a mission and together they set off across the fields towards the town.

They stuck to the hedgerows, keeping low. Woody was much faster than Ritchie. He could dig straight through hedges whilst Ritchie had to scramble as best he could, scramming his hands on nettles and wood.

'Blinkin' keep low and quiet,' hissed Woody.

Ritchie thought he was keeping low and quiet.

'They can smell you,' said Woody.

'Who?' panted Ritchie, who was struggling to keep up.

'All around. They are looking with their eyes.' Woody pointed to an oak tree. 'Up in the blinkin' branches – see their eyes.'

An owl swooped low between Woody and the tree, like a silent a drone. Ritchie gasped.

'Not the blinkin' owls,' hissed Woody. '*Behind* the owls.'

Ritchie scanned the tree as hard as he could, and then he saw them. Wide-eyed, two-legged creatures scuttling about on the beams and branches. 'What are they?'

'Night things, scary things – they robs you blind in the night – they've arrived here too. You people used to call them fairies – you know what I call them?'

Ritchie shook his head.

'Scaries,' said Woody. 'They creeps about in the night and nicks your best stuff. They're a blinkin' pain – watch 'em! They're following us.'

As Woody and Ritchie scuttled across the field, Ritchie could see more clearly now – a pack of little creatures holding sticks, running along behind them. Whenever he turned around, the creatures froze absolutely still and faded into the gloom.

They arrived at a wood next to the stream that led to the town.

'The Spannermen are camped in here – you've got to be quieter than a Scary,' said Woody.

They crept through the forest, passing the Spannermen. Ritchie never saw them, he just heard them snoring; they sounded like thousands of hospital breathing machines. There was a funny smell in the air. Ritchie sniffed it – it reminded him of the gun oil his dad used to clean his shotgun.

Finally, they came to the outskirts of the town, where the river meets the sea.

Here the glow of the streetlights gave them more to go by. Woody took Ritchie by the hand and led him to some stone outbuildings, falling down places, just off the main road to Cardigan.

'Shemi's in there,' said Woody, pointing to a small square stone building with no roof. 'It's an old pigsty.'

'Where's Doc and the Kid?'

Woody shrugged: 'Woody doesn't know everything.'

There was another stone building nearby – a crooked old cottage, with one window spilling yellow light. As they moved closer they could hear the sound of guitars being picked and singing. It was Doc Penfro and Kid Welly, strumming Country and Western music late into the night.

Ritchie and Woody clambered up the walls of the old pigsty and peeped in through the space where the slates used to be. Inside they saw Shemi, standing, head down, in a corner. There was a door, but it was locked. Ritchie clambered down and together he and Woody tried to force the door open. It wouldn't budge – but it made a lot of noise.

'Push it,' whispered Ritchie.

'Woody *is* blinkin' pushing,' hissed Woody. 'The blinkin' thing is locked like a shell.'

Neither of them noticed that the sound of music had stopped. They kept bashing on the door. Ritchie was the first to stop. He turned and looked at Doc and the Kid's building. The door opened and Doc and Kid stepped out.

'You hear summit?' asked Kid.

'Yeah,' said Doc. 'Better check the sheep.'

Doc and the Kid walked towards the pigsty, flashing a torch. Woody and Ritchie froze – they couldn't move because they'd be spotted – it was only a matter of seconds before they were discovered. Ritchie flipped his torch off, his finger catching on the switch as he flipped it off, causing it to fall to the floor. He closed his eyes half expecting Doc or Kid to hear the noise.

They didn't. They walked slowly towards the pigsty, flashing their own torch around.

Very gently, as the cowboys tramped over, Woody and Ritchie felt themselves being raised into the air. Thin furry arms, like monkey's arms, with soft hands and long fingernails, grabbed their shoulders and hoisted them silently up into the branches of a tree.

Ritchie was too scared to shout. As his feet disappeared into the foliage, Doc and the Kid walked straight past the spot he was standing on. Desperately he looked around. On the same branch he saw Woody, with a furry hand clamped across his mouth.

Beneath them Doc and the Kid unlocked the pigsty. They walked in.

Shemi the sheep took a step back. Doc shone the torch in his face. Kid asked the questions. 'OK sheep, we can do this the easy way, or we can do it the hard way. Tell us where the magic Blue Stone is?'

Shemi stared straight ahead, sliding his mouth from side to side, like he was chewing gum.

'We know you've been with Ritchie, the kid on the bus stop. We know Ritchie has found the Blue Stone. We know that he's a One Off because he understands the power of that special place. He's the only one who ever goes to that bus stop. Just tell us what he knows and we'll take you back to your field,' said Kid.

Shemi didn't move.

Doc flashed the light right in Shemi's face.

'Tell us, you dumb sheep! Tell us or we'll roast you up good and proper!' shouted Doc.

Shemi blinked in the bright light. But he didn't move. He didn't give anything away. He was a top level black sheep.

Above them, Ritchie watched in horror as Doc and Kid yelled at Shemi. Then he found himself on the move again.

13 Away

WOODY AND Ritchie were passed by the hands along the branches of what seemed like hundreds of trees. They were swung away from the pigsty, the old deserted cottage and the danger of Doc and Kid. Eventually the hands stopped. They let go of Woody first. He dropped to the forest floor with a splat. Then Ritchie joined him.

'What happened?' hissed Ritchie.

'Scaries,' explained Woody. 'We're really for it. They're probably going to spike us through with their sticky things.'

A Scary dropped from the tree – small, about the size of a dog, with big yellow eyes, long furry arms and feet shaped like claws. Other Scaries dropped down silently, landing on the ground like dust. You couldn't even hear them breathe.

'What d'you want?' asked Ritchie.

The first Scary tapped the ground with its claw.

'More to the point,' said the Scary, 'what do *you* want?'

Ritchie gasped at the sound of the Scary's voice. It was smooth, soft and it sang like a cat's purr, or a fly in the ear. It buzzed and tweaked the inside of his head. It made him bang his ears with the palms of his hands. It was as if someone was talking to him from inside.

Woody leant over to Ritchie. 'Don't talk to them and don't trust them; spill the beans and they'll spike you.'

But Ritchie couldn't see any point in not talking. After all, the Scaries had just, very gently, pulled him and Woody out of a very tricky situation. If the Scaries hadn't come at that moment they'd have been discovered by Doc and the Kid.

'We were trying to rescue the sheep,' said Ritchie.

Woody cried out with rage. 'Don't talk to them Scaries,' he shouted. 'Thousands of years of bad news are in the Scaries – stealing your stuff and making off with the best things.'

'Why?' asked the Scary, taking no notice of Woody.

'Because the sheep belongs to my friend,' said Ritchie.

The Scary nodded. 'Does the sheep know anything?' he asked.

Ritchie thought for a moment. He wasn't exactly sure how much Shemi the black sheep knew. 'Dunno,' he said. 'Sheep stuff, mainly. He hangs about by my bus stop.'

'We know,' said the Scary. 'But does he really know anything important? Does he know about the magic stone? Does he know that you are the one who discovered the ancient forces that spring from the earth at the cosmic intersection where you have built your bus stop? Does he know that the King has sent an army of Spannermen to find the missing rock? Does he know that if they find it, everything, even the Scaries, will stop?'

Ritchie didn't feel like saying that he hadn't actually built the bus stop himself – he just liked playing there.

'Does he know that you're a One Off because you're the human who discovered the spot?'

'I don't think so,' said Ritchie. 'I think he just wants to help.'

The Scaries were gathering around now, and there were more of them than before. Ritchie could see their yellow eyes peering down at them from the trees and he could see their furry bodies flitting in and out between the branches. But he couldn't hear them. They were totally silent – scary, he thought. Only one spoke.

'People don't like Scaries,' it said. 'We keep ourselves to ourselves. We live out of the way and we have our own rules.'

Woody shrank back – he hated Scaries. 'Spiky, sticky things are coming,' he warned.

'It's true. We dish it out to those who don't respect us, like this ditch-crawling little monster,' said the Scary, kicking Woody on the behind. 'But we aren't bad, we follow our law, we can tell good from wrong, and you, Ritchie, have been good. You talk to us without fear,' he said.

'That's 'cos he's nuts,' said Woody.

The Scary kicked Woody again.

'Not like you. We need something,' said the Scary, 'something that was lost thousands of years ago. A Blue Stone with tremendous power. This will protect us when the King arrives. This stone is here. But where? Does the sheep know? Will the sheep show it to the King?'

Ritchie shook his head. He was sure Shemi wanted the stone as much as anyone else. He was sure Shemi thought that *he* knew, and since Ritchie had absolutely no idea where the strange Blue Stone that everyone seemed to want was, he was sure Shemi had no idea either.

'No,' said Ritchie. 'Shemi doesn't know.'

'Only *you* know,' said the Scary. 'Or perhaps, only you *will* know. When the time comes – will you take us to the stone?'

Ritchie nodded. 'If I find it you'll be the first to know.'

A clanking sound – the rasping of metal on metal – interrupted their conversation. In silence, the Scaries began to disperse.

'Watch out on your way home,' warned the Scary. 'The King's Spannermen are here.' And without a sound, he vanished into the night.

Ritchie didn't have time to think. He grabbed Woody by the scruff of the neck and pulled him as hard as he could. There were more sounds – grinding metallic noises groaning louder – marching together.

'What you blinkin' doing?' shouted Woody.

'What's it look like,' yelled Ritchie. 'Run!'

Woody didn't need a second invitation.

They charged out of the forest and back into the fields. They could hear the sleeping Spannermen springing into life. The night air was filled with the crunch of rusty metal on metal. The last time Woody met the Spannermen they tried to eat him!

'Blinkin' Spannermen getting up now. Come on, Ritchie – get moving!' shouted Woody.

The journey back was the most frightening thing Ritchie had ever known. Metal arrows flew out of the black trees in the forest. Spannermen armed with rusty swords and clubs jumped out from the shadows, swinging their swords, axes and spiked metal clubs. But Woody and Ritchie were light and small enough to get past them. Once a Spannerman had grabbed Ritchie's foot, but Woody came back and smashed the Spannerman's hand so hard that it just fell apart. It was like a brick smashing an old clock.

'Thanks,' breathed Ritchie.

'Blinkin' silly boy, letting the creature take his foot,' muttered Woody as they ran.

Then, just as they reached the gate where Shemi

always stood during the day, and started climbing over, it happened. An arrow struck Woody. His arms shot up in the air and he flopped onto the ground on the wrong side of the gate. Ritchie had already jumped – he could see the bus stop and the main road just feet away. He turned to look for Woody.

'Go!' sighed Woody, from the gloom on the other side of the fence. 'They got me good and proper.'

Marching up the hill, Ritchie could see columns of Spannermen; he could hear their metal boots tramping like an army of robots. For a second, Ritchie hesitated. Woody was pointing at the bus stop, telling him to get away before the Spannermen killed him too. 'You can't be killed by the blinkin' stop,' whispered Woody. 'You've gotta find the blinkin' stone!'

A Spannerman jumped out of the dark and held his axe over Woody. Woody closed his eyes. Ritchie watched in horror as the rusty orange scrap metal figure raised his axe, a black toothed smile flashing across his frying pan face.

'No way!' shouted Ritchie.

Without thinking, Ritchie pitched himself back over the gate. He charged at the centre of the

Spannerman, headbutting his middle and knocking him back with clang. The Spannerman fell onto the muddy grass and struggled to regain his footing. Ritchie pulled Woody up and threw him over his shoulder and then he rushed to the gate. He bundled Woody over before leaping over the top bar himself. Then he dragged Woody into the bus stop.

'Woody's a gonner!' breathed Woody.

'What can I do?' asked Ritchie, aware of the fact that hedges and field boundaries all around were full of metal-eyed Spannermen.

'They won't come in here,' said Woody. 'This is an intersection.'

'I know – the Strumble Head flight path and the St David's to Cardigan bus route – but I don't see how it helps us, though,' said Ritchie.

'It's a magic place,' gasped Woody. 'Promise me you'll find the stone. If the Spannermen get it they'll give it to the King and it's curtains for us all.'

'Curtains?' asked Ritchie.

'Curtains,' said Woody. 'End of show.'

Woody closed his eyes. He lay perfectly still on the gravel in the bus stop, green blood oozing from the hole in his chest where the metal arrow had gone in. Ritchie searched desperately for someone to help them, but the road was silent, almost silver in the dim starlight. As he paced up and down the bus stop, he tried to think what his dad would have done in the army.

Ritchie stood by the entrance of the bus stop and yelled at the top of his voice. 'Man down!' He remembered that his dad had told him this is what they said if someone was hit. You shouted, and because you were with your mates, because you were with your unit, if anyone was out there they'd come and help. That's what Jamie's mates did for him in Helmand. It was like a special emergency call, only to be used when someone was hit.

'Man down!' shouted Ritchie again, running into the empty road.

'MAN DOWN!'

He screamed into the blank, silent night. Then he stopped shouting. He realised that he was in the middle of nowhere. His bus stop was about as far from help as it could be. It was the bus stop at the end of the world. He looked back at Woody, lying bleeding in the bus stop.

'Man down,' he sighed and ran back into the bus stop to see if there was anything to do.

But Woody had lost consciousness. Ritchie crouched on his knees and listened to Woody's chest. He couldn't hear a heartbeat. Tears filled his eyes. 'Woody,' he gasped, 'come back!'

'Can I help?'

A familiar voice disturbed Ritchie. Without thinking he said: 'No.'

Then Ritchie turned to see that it was the Woolly Woman in the brown coat. Ritchie looked around desperately, trying to work out how she'd got there.

'I heard you call,' she said. 'Although I must say, I'm very cross with you for waking me up in the middle of the night.'

'I'm sorry,' said Ritchie. 'It's just that my friend's been shot.'

'Clearly,' said the old lady, grabbing the arrow with both her hands and pulling as hard as she could. With a shudder it slid out. Ritchie tried to peep below the brim of her hat. He thought he saw a face, but it was very indistinct; it was like looking for a mouse in the cupboard under the stairs.

'Hmmm,' said the Woolly Woman, inspecting the metal arrow as if it was a dirty fork from a washing machine. 'You're friend's got green blood.'

'I know,' said Ritchie 'Is that bad?'

'No,' said the old woman, resting her hand on Woody's forehead. 'It's just a rather unusual blood group. Blood group green – now that *is* in short supply.'

'Will he be OK?' asked Ritchie.

'Fixing old-time creatures like this isn't easy for me,' said the old woman. 'I haven't come across a troll for years and years.'

'What's a troll?' asked Ritchie.

The Woolly Woman looked at Ritchie as if to say, 'Don't be so stupid'.

'Sorry,' said Ritchie, looking at Woody. 'I guess this is a troll.'

Woody sighed and shivered on the floor of the bus stop. His eyelids flickered.

The old lady stood, she looked around the bus stop. 'Spannermen all around! When's the next bus due in?'

'Seven thirty a.m. to Aberystwyth,' replied Ritchie. 'First of the day.'

'We've got time,' said the old lady.

'What for?' asked Ritchie.

'I need some curtains,' she said, rummaging in her bag. Ritchie stared into the night, mouthing the word 'curtains' to himself. How could she think about decorating at a time like this?

'Wait outside, please,' said the old lady, producing white sheets from her handbag and sticking them up on the inside of the bus stop with sellotape.

'I'm going to have to operate,' she explained. 'You'll have to keep guard. You're a human – you can't know anything about trolls. You mustn't know anything about me and you shouldn't be allowed to witness any of my special techniques. If the Spannermen interrupt the delicate surgery, your little troll won't make it.'

As she spoke, the Woolly Woman kept pulling more and more sheets from her handbag. She was like a children's wizard with hankies, thought Ritchie. Except this was no trick. She was turning the bus stop into a kind of hospital.

'Will he be all right?' asked Ritchie, as he stepped out into the road.

'I don't know,' replied the Woolly Woman, pulling a ball of wool, candles and some knitting needles from her bag. 'He's been shot through the heart with a rusty arrow. It's not good. But trolls are strong and they're quite easy to stitch up. You may have noticed – your friend isn't very complicated, is he?'

Ritchie nodded. As far as he could see there was nothing complicated about Woody whatsoever.

She put the finishing touches to the curtains which now surrounded the inside of the bus stop and pulled the flap shut.

Ritchie waited on the roadside outside the hospital. He knew the Spannermen were watching him, but they were too scared to come too close to the bus stop. He stood by the entrance and ventured once to ask the Woolly Woman how it was going.

She popped her head around the corner; she had tied a candle to the top of her head with a scarf. 'Be quiet, keep guard and don't ask stupid questions,' she said.

Ritchie said sorry. He was just worried about Woody. He stood sentry, searching for Spannermen. The hedgerows clinked and clanked, the trees groaned like a straining ship, but the Spannermen weren't brave enough to venture out into the light.

Finally, after what seemed hours, the Woolly Woman stepped out of the field hospital. 'You can come in now!'

Ritchie went in. The room was bathed in white light shining from the candles and reflecting from the sheets. Woody lay on the floor. The old lady wore a white gown and a mask. She snapped her yellow rubber gloves off.

'I told you my powers aren't what they were,' she said. 'A few years ago I could have revived him using a spell, but now I've only been able to do a little magic – enough to make everything safe. I couldn't find any troll's blood in my handbag. In the end I used a spinach smoothie.'

'Thanks,' said Ritchie.

'He's fine,' she said, tracing her finger down the long scar that divided Woody's chest in half. 'All this will fade away in the next few minutes. By the morning he won't even know he was hit.' The old lady sat down on the bus stop floor underneath the words: "Do as we say or the sheep gets it."

Ritchie sat down next to her. 'What are you doing?' she asked.

'Waiting for Woody to wake up,' replied Ritchie.

'You go home,' she said. 'I'll make sure the Spannermen don't take him. And then I've really got to catch that 7.30 to Aberystwyth.'

14 The deal

THE NEXT day was tough for Ritchie. He kept falling asleep in school. The Collins gang called him 'Dozy Ritchie Ritch', and everybody laughed at him.

Ritchie didn't care at all, though. He had much bigger things on his mind. He'd worked out a way of saving Shemi. He would ask Woody to dig a tunnel.

When Ritchie arrived at the bus stop after school he went straight to the hedge and called Woody.

Woody appeared, looking sorry for himself. 'What a bad plan that blinkin' was,' he said, rubbing the stitches on his chest.

'No worries,' said Ritchie, 'I've got a better one now. We'll dig Shemi out.'

Woody nodded, stroking his chin. Then he must have heard something, because he dived back into the hedge. Ritchie spun around to see Annie Bike skidding to a halt at the stop. She jumped off her bike and asked Ritchie if he'd seen Shemi. She was in a real state, and her eyes were blotchy because she'd been crying. Shemi was her favourite sheep; he was her special pet. Ritchie bit his lip as he made his way back to the bus stop. He realised he'd have to tell Annie what had happened – everything. He couldn't pretend he didn't know Shemi was being interrogated by the cowboys, Doc and Kid. He just didn't think she'd believe him.

'Annie,' said Ritchie.

'What,' asked Annie. 'Do you know something?'

Ritchie nodded. 'I can help,' he said. 'But you've got to believe me.'

'Why shouldn't I?' asked Annie.

'Because what I'm going to tell you isn't going to sound very likely. In fact, you'll think I'm making it up. But I've found Shemi – that's the important thing.'

A broad smile of relief spread across Annie's face. She grabbed Ritchie and hugged him. Then she started dancing around the bus stop. 'Come on – what are we waiting for? Let's fetch him.'

'It's not as simple as that. Read this,' said Ritchie, pointing at the writing on the bus timetable.

'Do as we say,' said the message, 'or the sheep gets it. Yours respectfully, Doc and the Kid.'

Annie read, her blue-green eyes opening wide. 'Who are Doc and the Kid? What's going on, Ritchie? Is Shemi OK?'

'You'd better sit down,' said Ritchie.

Together they sat on the floor of the bus stop and Ritchie began to tell Annie everything he knew. In the end it was difficult to leave anything out. He told her about a small green man called Woody, about Doc Penfro and Kid Welly, and about how he and Woody had found Shemi in a disused pigsty near town. He told her about the Blue Stone and the fact that the entire underworld seemed to be trying to find it, and they all seemed to think that he knew where it was. He told her that everyone thought he was a One Off and that he was the one who stole the stone in the first place.

'I'm getting my dad,' said Annie. 'He'll blast them.'

Ritchie grabbed her arm. 'No!' he exclaimed. 'I said you've got to believe me. These people are weird. Your dad might end up in serious trouble. I can get the sheep back myself.'

Annie looked at Ritchie. She didn't quite see what he could do that her dad couldn't. 'My dad'll kill them, I'm telling you,' she said, leaping to her feet.

'You've got to believe me,' pleaded Ritchie. 'It's absolutely essential that you do – your dad even with his farmer's gun wouldn't stand a chance against this lot. They're all around us. They're probably watching us now. I mean, seriously, they've got much more firepower than your dad. You've got to believe me.'

'So where is it?' said Annie, not believing a word.

'The stone or the sheep?' asked Ritchie.

'The stone,' said Annie.

'I don't know,' shouted Ritchie, jumping to his feet. He rushed outside the bus stop and shouted at the crow. 'I don't know where it is. How am I supposed to know?'

The crow turned its head away, and as Annie hurried out to try and calm Ritchie down, it focused on something crawling up the hill from town. It was the 245 for St Davids. Unusually, it stopped at the bus stop. Two men hopped off, one of them carrying a large black sack on his back.

Ritchie jabbed Annie in the ribs. 'Hide! It's them!'

Annie skipped behind the stop and hit the floor.

'Howdee, Ritchie Rich,' said Doc, plonking the sack down on the floor. It bleated.

Kid stepped up to Ritchie, eyeing him menacingly. 'The time for talking's over,' he said.

'Is it?' asked Ritchie.

Doc held out his dad's army torch. 'Did you lose something last night, boy?'

Ritchie took the torch – his dad had stuck a label with his name and address on it. He didn't say anything.

'You know what we've got in that bag?' asked Kid.

Ritchie could guess, so he nodded slowly. He told Doc and Kid that he and Woody had found their hide-out.

'We figured as much,' said Kid. 'We smelt that little trench digger friend of yours. Now, if you want this black sheep back, you tell us where that stone is.'

There was another bleat from the bag, as if Shemi was telling Ritchie not to speak.

Ritchie was just about to say something very clever when, bam! Annie flew at Doc's head from behind the bus stop. She shot out, punching and kicking and cursing, causing Doc to fall backwards, and then she turned and began tearing at the sack. Shemi started kicking and bleating too.

Ritchie shook his head. Annie's attack was very brave, but it wasn't going to work. Doc and Kid were too big. As Ritchie ran to help her, Kid grabbed him and pinned him to the timetable. Doc recovered his footing and grabbed Annie, covering her mouth with his hand.

'I've a mind to toss all three of you into the ocean,' said Doc. 'Now will you show us the stone?'

Ritchie surveyed the scene: a black sheep in a black bag, Annie trying to gnaw her way through Doc's hand and the whiskey-smelling Kid Welly gripping his shoulders like a vice. There was nothing for it. He nodded slowly, gravely pushing Kid's hands off. Annie's eyes opened still wider. She had no idea what Ritchie was going to do, but he seemed to have some kind of plan.

Woody, who was hiding in the hedge, watched and muttered to himself: 'This is Woody's chance in a thousand years. Woody be quiet, Woody be cool, watch for the stone.'

Ritchie began to move slowly away from the bus stop. He walked to the gate and at the stone field boundaries, he passed his hands slowly over the rocks, as if sensing the power. Just to add a bit of mystery to the process he started to hum a tune to himself. They were just random notes, but he made them sound like some kind of witchcraft curse. His heart was pounding; if his bluff didn't work he reckoned that he, Shemi and Annie could all end up dead. He closed his eyes – he needed some words – some magical sounding words. Then he began to make up words:

> 'Blue Stone of Power,
> Wherever you are,
> Near or far,
> Far or ... not so far.'

Ritchie paused for a second, waving his hands around. He couldn't think of any other words that rhymed with 'far'. 'Car' was no good because that was too modern.

Kid Welly and Doc Penfro exchanged glances –

now it was their turn to wonder about Ritchie. Was he making it up as he went along?

Annie Bike knew they were thinking this. She wanted shout out, to help Ritchie. 'Star' was a great word – it rhymed with 'far' and it had something to do with magic and stuff like that.

'Far or not so far,' repeated Ritchie, then louder: 'Far or not so far.'

He stopped, his hands trembling over a huge boulder about the size of two sheep, embedded deep in the stone field boundary. 'You are the star!' he shouted, pointing to the stone.

Annie sighed with relief – Ritchie was telepathic as well as being a magician!

'That's it,' said Ritchie, pointing at the stone.

Doc and the Kid looked at each other. The crow hopped down from the roof of the bus stop for a closer look, and even Woody broke his cover and stepped out into the light.

Kid bent down next to the stone, sniffing it with his big fat nose, his moustache flicking its surface.

'Don't smell magic,' he said. 'Don't look so blue either.'

'If the stone was actually coloured bright blue

you wouldn't need me to help you find it, would you?' said Ritchie impatiently, as he began untying Shemi's bag. Shemi stuck his head out, and just for a second Annie thought the sheep winked at Ritchie with his strange letterbox eyes. Annie threw herself around Shemi's neck.

'Don't feel so magic to me,' said Doc, rubbing the stone.

'What do you expect?' asked Ritchie. 'Rabbits and top hats? I'm telling you, that's your stone, like the lady said – it's here at this bus stop. That's why I'm here. *I'm* here because *it*'s here; I'm here to look after it.'

Doc let go of Annie, pulled the black sheep out of its sack and practically threw it over the gate. Annie ran to Shemi, who stamped his feet and shook his fleece, trying to restore his dignity. Eventually he walked up to the gate and began doing what he was best at – looking down his long nose at humans. Annie hugged him.

Doc and Kid inspected the stone in the field boundary. Ritchie had picked a big one; they decided they needed shovels to dig it out and hurried off to town to find some.

Woody watched and waited as the sun set

behind the Boggy Hills. Eventually, Ritchie and Annie walked away up the Winding Lane. Ritchie complained about having to do reading with his dad. Annie talked non-stop about Shemi, the cowboys and her sheep. She said she'd tell her dad about Doc and the Kid, and he'd be down with his shotgun to shoot them for sheep rustling. When she did finally ask about the Blue Stone and how Ritchie knew it was there, he confessed. He told Annie that he simply picked the biggest rock he could find. It wasn't his fault if everyone thought he had magic powers. The only definite thing he could say about the boulder he'd identified was that it was big – very big.

Nightfall twinkled on the bus stop. The crow perched on the roof and watched the road by moonlight. Occasionally a car would speed past. Eventually two men appeared. Doc and the Kid had found some shovels. As they approached, the blades of their tools clinked on the tarmac. They talked. The crow listened.

'What a fine night for bit of serious digging,' said Doc, as he approached the stone. 'Grave digging, even.'

'We take the stone and then take the first bus

out of here,' said Kid. 'There's too many spooks around, and then when we're safe.'

'How far do we need to go to be safe?' asked Doc, pushing his shovel into the ground.

'A long way,' replied Kid Welly. 'Maybe as far away as Swansea.'

'Good, I like the plan – lay low, keep quiet and then slowly we use the stone. The King'll never find us in Swansea,' said Doc.

Kid started digging fast, his shovel clanging the side of the rock. 'One thing,' he said. 'How do we use this stone? How do we turn it on?'

Doc looked at Kid as if he was an idiot. 'It's five thousand years old; it hasn't got a dimmer switch. There will be a way – a spell, an incantation – you heard the boy. Maybe you have to heat it up … we'll find a way. The first thing we've got to do is get it away from here.'

They dug for hours. Woody watched them with a broad smile on his face from a hiding place in the hedge. He'd checked underground – the stone was like a tooth, its roots went deep into the earth, only the tip broke the surface. There was no way Doc and Kid were going to get to the bottom of it and no way that they would be able to carry it from there. The crow watched. Occasionally the two men would pause, mopping their brows, blowing hot air into the cold, damp, silver air. Shemi watched too, his yellow eyes shining like fires in the black soot of his fleece.

'It's no good,' admitted Kid, leaning on his shovel. 'This stone's as big as a house. We'll have to come back with a digger.'

Doc wanted to get on with the job, but he could see from the size of the hole that they'd already dug that the stone was too big to pull out and too heavy to carry. He pushed his hat back on his head and raised his eyes to the starry night. Starlight flickered in the beads of sweat on his forehead. He looked at Kid, panting and wheezing over his shovel. He was still digging as hard as he could. 'Stop, Kid,' he sighed. 'What we have here requires mechanised equipment.'

Kid carried on digging, obsessed by the idea of taking the stone. But Doc put his hand on Kid's back and told him to put his shovel down. He told Kid that he knew how important it was to get to the stone, to guarantee them safety as the forces of darkness gradually spread out across the world. But the stone was just too big.

Reluctantly Kid and Doc walked back to the town. They agreed that at sunrise they'd return with mechanised equipment.

As they disappeared down the road and out of view, something strange began to happen. The stone, massive though it was, began to shake.

15 The witch

RITCHIE RUSHED down to the bus stop early the next morning, biting through his lucky red sweet and swallowing it quickly. Even though it was early he'd found his dad in the kitchen, drinking coffee and looking out across the dewy fields as the sun came up. Ritchie couldn't decide if Jamie had been up all night or whether he'd just put on the same clothes as he'd been wearing the day before. Jamie said Ritchie was doing well with his reading and together they sat down and read a story in yesterday's newspaper about a football manager who was getting sacked. Ritchie concentrated as hard as he could and read as fast as possible because he really wanted to go to the bus stop. He realised, as he said some of the smaller words, that he was beginning to read almost as fast as his dad. If he beat Jamie, Jamie laughed out loud, saying things like: 'Nice one, Ritchie!' When they'd finished the story, Jamie told Ritchie that he was a good kid and he was getting better at reading, then he gave him the red sweet.

Ritchie ran down the Winding Lane and tumbled out onto the bus stop. He had a feeling something important would be there, but when he arrived, he found nothing, or perhaps less than nothing; because, although the bus stop was empty, there was a huge hole next to it in the ground where the stone once was. Ritchie walked to the hole – it was big enough for a tall man to stand in and not be seen. He figured that Doc and Kid had managed somehow to lever the stone out and roll it down the hill. But strangely, when he looked for tracks, there were none.

'You'll be needing another tenner soon,' a soft voice trickled into Ritchie's ear.

Behind him stood two familiar figures – the tall thin lady and the short fat one.

'For school,' smiled the older, thinner one.

Ritchie had almost forgotten about school.

The tall thin woman was dressed in black and wrapped in a veil of morning mist, as if she'd walked out of the dawn. She held out a ten pound note in her thin hand. Her skin was dry – just like the ten pound note.

Ritchie didn't take the money, although he wanted to.

'Just tell me where the *real* stone is,' said the stranger with a smile.

Shemi walked up to the gate and watched, shaking his head slightly.

'That *was* the real stone,' said Ritchie unconvincingly.

'No stone, no money,' said the woman, handing the note to her assistant who smiled and placed it in a black purse, snapping it shut with a fierce 'click'.

'Have a think, Ritchie, today when you're in school. You could do with a tenner. Your dad's got no money so he can't help you, and those boys – what are their names?'

'The Collins gang,' muttered Ritchie. 'Psychic, Delaney and Collins – obviously.'

'Exactly. Those boys, they're expecting a payment. And of course, there is another thing you have to consider.'

'What?' asked Ritchie, reluctantly.

'If you don't take the money and lead me to the Blue Stone, I can have you burned alive.'

Ritchie took a step back. The girl, who wasn't much older than Ritchie, guarded the purse and smiled broadly revealing a single gold front tooth. She seemed to like the idea of burning Ritchie alive.

'You can't do that,' said Ritchie. 'Not here, not at my bus stop. It's against the law – you'd get done.'

'I would if I wasn't quite so powerful. I can travel in time and space, I can call up an army of spirits from the underworld ...'

'The Spannermen?' asked Ritchie.

'Don't interrupt, boy – I've never heard of them. I'm talking about goblins, elves, spirits and of course, my dragon.'

Ritchie laughed. The woman sounded half mad. She walked around the bus stop, her tight little black shoes scraping the ground like knives. Ritchie noticed the crow take off and flap away into a distant tree.

'I'll be waiting for you,' said the strange thin woman. 'In the meantime, you see that tree the crow has just hidden in?'

Ritchie nodded. The crow was perched in a

chestnut tree, its leaves spreading out like great green hands in the morning light.

'Watch.'

To say Ritchie's jaw hit the floor would be an understatement. What he saw knocked him back like a punch. The tree blew up. Or perhaps it just caught fire and burned to a cinder very quickly. One minute it was standing there, all quiet, conkers ready to drop and green; the next it was ablaze with flames; and then, in an instant, it was just a thick black stalk, smoking slightly.

'Nice work, Bertie,' said the woman.

The bus trundled down to the stop. Ritchie completely forgot to put his hand out. He just jumped on and rushed to a seat.

'Everything all right?' asked Gloria.

Ritchie couldn't speak, and as the bus pulled off Ritchie noticed a big yellow digger motoring up the hill. Doc Penfro was driving, Kid Welly was sitting in the shovel.

Gloria looked at Ritchie. Her eyes strayed off the road and into her mirrors for just one second. Ritchie saw her. She felt the need to say something. 'That old woman in black, and that short fat girl ...'

'Yes?' said Ritchie, looking at Gloria.

Gloria blushed, as if she was saying something she shouldn't. 'I'm not one to gossip,' she said.

'I know,' said Ritchie, 'nor am I.'

'But you know who that was.'

'No,' said Ritchie.

'I really shouldn't say,' said Gloria. Then she added: 'But I will.'

As they drove to school, Gloria told Ritchie about Mrs Penfold and her mean granddaughter, Rhiannon. Gloria said that they were well known around town for being "weird". She told Ritchie that he should not bother with them because people thought that she was into black magic. She said that they put curses on people and bad things happened to them. Gloria went on to say that once Mrs Penfold had put a curse on one of the buses she was driving, and almost as soon as Mrs Penfold had stepped off (without paying), all four tyres had burst.

16 Show down

IN SCHOOL, Ritchie saw Miss Croons and read for her. She said he was doing "very well", although Ritchie knew he wasn't doing well at all; all he could think about were exploding trees, disappearing rocks and a strange feeling that everything he knew – his cottage, the buses, the school, the whole lot – was starting to fall apart, as if it didn't mean anything at all. He ran into the Collins gang who said it was time for their next payment.

At the end of the day when Ritchie stepped off the bus and onto the tarmac, he hoped things would be back to normal. But when he looked at the crow, who was back on his perch on the roof of the bus stop, he could see that things weren't right. The bird's feathers were burned and singed and there were little bald patches on its wings.

It had obviously only just managed to flap away from the tree before the dragon burned it.

Ritchie walked to the gate. Shemi chewed his grass, hardly bothering to acknowledge Ritchie. There was a sound.

'Pssst.'

Ritchie looked around. He couldn't see anyone – no witches, no Country and Western singers. Then he looked down at the ground and saw two eyes peering up at him from the earth, one blue, one black. It was Woody. With a little wriggle, Woody was up on the ground. He danced around on the road in front of Ritchie. 'If you can dig you can groove,' he laughed. 'Woody's got the stone.'

'What?' shouted Ritchie.

'Woody can dig. He waits for the cowboys to get tired with their stupid spades. Then, when they goes down, Woody pulls the stone down into the ground. Woody's got the stone now. Nobody can hurt him because he's got the magic boulder. Blinkin' enormous it is. The size of a blinkin' bus.'

'Where did you hide it?' asked Ritchie.

'Under the ground,' said Woody, with a knowing wink of his big blue eye.

'And that means you think you're safe,' said Ritchie, 'when the King comes and spreads darkness all over the world, when he pulls everything apart, every single living thing. You think you're safe because you've got that rock? How can you hide a rock under the ground?'

'Easy for Woody,' shouted Woody as he laughed and danced. 'Woody is in his oils under the ground.' He cackled and rubbed his leathery green hands together and held his sides when he laughed about Doc Penfro and Kid Welly's attempt to use a mechanical digger to find the stone.

'Blinkin' super-funny,' said Woody. 'When those two cowboys arrive with their digger and find the stone the size of a bus has gone into the air, they'll scratch their heads and they can't understand. They swears and fights like dogs and cats. They think it's all the magic of the King and the coming of darkness to the world. But Woody knows it's the magic of knowing how to dig holes what got the rock off its spot.'

Ritchie sighed. He knew there was nothing unusual about the stone, apart from its size. Ritchie found himself looking out to sea, as dragon-shaped clouds flipped across the blue sky. Suddenly Woody stopped dancing and froze. He'd heard something. As Annie Bike zoomed up, Woody slid back down into the ground.

'Wait,' shouted Ritchie, but Woody had gone.

'Ritchie, what's going on?' shouted Annie. 'I saw those boys in school today. What did they want?'

'Nothing really,' lied Ritchie.

'Are they bullying you?' she asked. 'Because if they are, I'll get dad to shoot them as well as the sheep rustlers! He's in a bad mood at the moment.'

'Look Annie,' said Ritchie, 'I've got to tell you about something.'

Ritchie told Annie about the witch, the dragon, Woody and the magic stone. Annie listened carefully; she'd seen enough to know that something unusual was going on because the town was filling up with strangers. But she still couldn't quite believe that it wasn't to do with sheep rustling. Her dad thought that the place was filling up with sheep stealers. Ritchie tried to explain that it was bigger than that. He tried to explain that all everybody wanted was the magic stone.

'Well,' said Annie, after listening to Ritchie's story, 'you'd better find it.'

Ritchie laughed. 'How am I supposed to do that?

I can't even read, I don't know anybody round here and you're right, when I go to school everybody laughs at me, beats me up and takes my money off me. I'm special all right. I'm specially rubbish. I'm a One Off at doing things wrong.'

Annie's eyes flashed with rage. She slapped Ritchie really hard across the face. It hurt Ritchie. 'Don't be such a sap,' she yelled. '*You*'re not rubbish; *they*'re all rubbish! What makes you rubbish is believing them. You know what I think? I think you made half of this stuff up just so you don't have to sort out the really important things.'

Ritchie felt his face. It went red, partly where Annie had slapped it, and partly where she hadn't. He didn't know what to say, he felt like crying.

'I'm sorry,' said Annie.

'It's OK,' said Ritchie. 'I deserved it.'

Annie sighed. 'No you didn't deserve it – the others are the ones who deserve a good kicking. Give it to the Collins gang. Beat 'em up!' she shouted.

As Ritchie listened to Annie, thinking to himself that taking on the Collins gang was a good idea in principle, but a very bad one in reality, he noticed her face change. From full of anger, she'd gone to full of fear. She held up her hand, pointing at two figures who were tramping up the hill – Doc Penfro and Kid Welly. They had thunderous faces. Ritchie grabbed Annie, pulling her out of the bus stop. The two men were now running straight at them. There was nothing for it. Ritchie and Annie tore out of the bus stop and started sprinting up the First Hill. Doc and the Kid chased after them, shouting about the missing stone and how they'd beat the location of the magic stone out of Ritchie.

As they ran, Annie turned to Ritchie and shouted: 'You know, Ritchie, the first thing you have got to do is find that stone!'

'And what's the second?' asked Ritchie, panting as his feet pounded the road.

'Get rid of it!' yelled Annie. 'Hide it good and proper so that nobody bothers you ever again.'

A bus appeared at the top of the hill – the 479 to Cardigan. Ritchie could hear Doc and Kid puffing up behind them. They were gaining ground. As he ran, Ritchie tried to think what his dad would have done to get out of trouble – something special, something unusual, something brave. Suddenly Ritchie had an idea. He knew what to do – he was a One Off, after all. He swerved straight out into the middle of the road and stood in front of the oncoming bus. Annie covered her eyes; she thought Ritchie was bound to be flattened by the front of the Volvo City Bus. Even Doc and Kid stopped and watched in horror as the driver slammed on the brakes, causing the wheels to lock and screech, and the big Firestone tyres to pour out clouds of choking smoke. The driver was a good one. It was Mr Dickinson. Ritchie knew Mr Dickinson would have great brakes on his rig. Skilfully, Mr Dickinson brought the sky-blue bus to a standstill, inches in front of Ritchie. Ritchie ran to the side of the bus, waving as Mr Dickinson opened the doors just long enough for Annie and Ritchie to leap on. Then the bus started and the doors swung closed as they began driving down the hill past the cowboys. Annie smiled and waved as Doc and Kid shook their fists at the windows.

'Friends of yours?' asked Mr Dickinson, looking down at Doc and Kid.

'Not exactly,' said Ritchie, taking a seat next to Annie in the middle of the bus.

The lady in the seat in front of them turned and put her head over the headrest – Annie expected her to shush them up. But it wasn't just any old passenger. Ritchie recognised her instantly – that ten-pound-note-crinkly-paper-skin and that pasty-faced-gold-tooth-oil-eyed partner of hers popped their heads up like a couple of balloons.

'I think we've gone far enough,' said Mrs Penfold. 'Let's get off at this stop.'

'Don't give us any trouble,' added Rhiannon.

Annie was just going to argue with them when Ritchie jabbed her in the side with his elbow. He'd seen the tree go up in smoke so he knew just how powerful Mrs Penfold was. She was an old school witch, and you didn't mess with those. Mrs Penfold nodded at Mr Dickinson and he dutifully set them all down back at the bus stop. Before leaving the bus, Ritchie thanked Mr Dickinson for stopping, and explained that the old lady was Annie's grandmother and that they were visiting her parents at her farm. Mr Dickinson nodded and smiled. He liked Ritchie, but he had no idea what he was up to, and in his wing mirrors he could see Doc and the Kid charging back down the hill. Without asking any questions, Mr Dickinson slipped his bus into first gear and away from the bus stop and out of harm's way.

Mrs Penfold spat on the ground by the bus. A little plume of smoke hissed up from the spot where her spit hit the tarmac. She gestured towards the bus stop and slowly they stepped inside. Ritchie could see Doc and Kid jogging breathlessly back down the road. Finally, Doc, followed by Kid, stumbled, breathless, into the bus stop.

'You pesky varmint!' snarled Kid. 'Where 'ave you put the stone?'

Ritchie watched Doc and the Kid, hands on hips, puffing breathlessly. They seriously believed that he'd moved the stone – the bus-sized stone!

Mrs Penfold and Rhiannon, her assistant, glared at Ritchie. They seemed to believe the same thing.

Annie looked at Ritchie too, knowing that he couldn't have moved the stone.

But Ritchie thought quickly. Instead of telling them what really happened, he pretended. After all, the reason why the witch, the cowboys, the crow and the King himself were interested in Ritchie was the fact that they thought he had special powers. Pretending he had special powers wasn't so difficult.

'Nice trick with the dragon this morning, Mrs Penfold,' said Ritchie.

Annie smiled. She knew Ritchie was going to talk them both out of trouble.

'I haven't seen a fire like that for some time,' added Ritchie. 'You very nearly toasted the crow.'

There was a 'caw' from outside.

Mrs Penfold nodded, politely accepting the compliment.

Doc Penfro and Kid Welly looked sweaty and uncomfortable, but they nodded in agreement as they panted for breath. Everybody stared at Ritchie. He smiled and took a position in front of the timetable, explaining that he had hidden the stone. And, by referring to the bus times, the flight paths overhead and anything else he could think of that made his intersection special, he told them how he'd hidden the magic Blue Stone, for everyone's safety.

'We need to trust one another,' he said, 'so that the stone doesn't fall into the wrong hands.'

He told everybody that the best thing to do would be for them to gather together all the creatures – beings, ghosts and mythological characters who were searching for the magical stone. He could explain to them all that this was the best way for them to protect themselves and everybody else against the arrival of the King.

'The King is on his way,' shouted Ritchie. 'We must be prepared. Down with the King!'

To Ritchie's amazement, everybody in the

bus stop nodded. There was even an echo. 'Down with the King,' repeated his audience, nervously.

Mrs Penfold asked Rhiannon to unclip the black purse and hand the ten pound note to Ritchie. 'For good behaviour.'

Doc Penfro and Kid Welly left first. They walked out of the bus stop, shaking Ritchie by the hand.

'You're a One Off, Ritchie,' said Doc Penfro. 'We'll rustle up a posse and then you can take us to the stone.'

Ritchie nodded, slightly awkwardly.

'No problem' said Annie, confidently. 'Ritchie's got everything covered.'

Mrs Penfold and Rhiannon were the next to leave. Mrs Penfold smiled and told Ritchie she'd put the word out; she knew thousands of witches who wanted to see the Blue Stone.

Ritchie nodded.

'Now,' she said, 'seeing as you're one of us, you won't mind if I give Bertie a call.'

'Bertie?' asked Annie.

'Bertie's her dragon,' explained Ritchie. 'He blows things up.'

'He's a pretty good flier too,' said Mrs Penfold, whistling with her fingers between her teeth.

'Most dragons are pretty slow, dinosaur type creatures, but Bertie – he's like a cross between a Lamborghini and a cruise missile.'

Before Annie and Ritchie had time to catch their breath, they were knocked back by a gust of wind and the tremendous roar of a sonic boom, as Bertie flew straight down from the sky. He didn't skid to a halt. He kind of roared onto the spot.

Annie and Ritchie shrank back. Bertie was fierce. Scorched red in colour, he was about the size of a horse. He was covered in black soot marks from his fiery mouth, had steely scales and smelled like burned coal. Bertie glared around, his eyes as bright as diamonds, smoke billowing from his mouth.

'Would you like to see another explosion?' asked Mrs Penfold eagerly. 'You see that house half way up the hill?'

The dragon fixed its eyes on the cottage.

'Shall we nuke it?'

'Nooooo!' yelled Ritchie, 'I live there – my dad's in there!'

'Shame,' said Mrs Penfold hopping onto the dragon's back and pulling Rhiannon up behind her. 'Bertie likes a bit of target practice.'

With that, Bertie was gone, straight upwards,

0–1400 miles an hour in one second. All that was left was just a whiff of black smoke and the crisp smell of freshly hewn coal.

Annie sat down. 'I thought you were a strange kind of kid,' she said, 'playing in here all the time on your own. But you're not. What's going on?'

'I've got to get that stone back,' moaned Ritchie.

'But it's not really magic,' said Annie.

'I know, but they all think it is. They think this bus stop sits on the intersection of cosmic ley lines and that this is where the magic stone is. Worse still, they think I'm a One Off. They think that thousands of years ago I stole the Blue Stone. I couldn't tell the difference between a magic stone and a normal one – could you?'

Annie paused. 'Maybe it shines, or bleeps, or warms up and kind of pulsates,' she said, shaking her head.

'Don't think so. Shining, bleeping, pulsating stones would be too easy to find,' said Ritchie sadly.

'I thought you were a One Off,' she said. 'I mean … really.'

Ritchie looked at Annie as if she was the one who'd lost the plot. 'Do I look like one of them? I'm an ordinary kid, like you.' Ritchie hesitated. 'Well ... not like you, I can't ride a bike like you, I can't read like you, I can't do sport like you.'

'No,' said Annie, 'but there *is* something about you. They're right. You are a bit of a One Off – maybe not a magic One Off, but I've never met anyone else who can really talk to dragons, I mean, really.'

Ritchie nodded. That much was true. He was the only person he knew who could honestly say that he'd told a dragon not to blow up his dad.

'Can't you just ... tune in?' asked Annie. 'Can't you just tune in to the special stone by using your special powers? I mean, they're right – there's lots of ancient legends about the stones around here. Maybe there's something in it.'

'How?' asked Ritchie.

'Think – with your special One Off mind. Close your eyes and think about the cosmic ley lines, the bus stop, the energy in the earth – all that hippy stuff,' said Annie.

Ritchie closed his eyes and tried to tune into the earth. He held the palms of his hands out flat. He held his breath.

Eventually, he had to breathe. With a big burst he opened his mouth and blew out and in, panting and shaking his head, laughing. 'Nothing,' he said. 'Absolutely rock bottom nothing.'

17 The attack of the Spannermen

RITCHIE AND Annie walked up the Winding Lane towards their houses. Annie pushed her bike, still talking about the dragons, witches and other characters Ritchie had introduced her to. Ritchie made her promise not to tell anyone.

'Wait a minute,' she said. 'What about Shemi?'

Ritchie laughed at Annie. Her big blue-green eyes blinked at him, a bit like Shemi's, he thought.

Ritchie told her that Shemi the sheep was safe because Shemi knew what was going on, just like the crow. He left Annie and walked up the Winding Lane that led to his cottage. The Rover was parked on a patch of grass outside the rickety wooden door. All around were bits of old trailers, tyres from tractors, and other pieces of farm equipment. Ritchie shoved the door open and stepped into the living room. Jamie was sitting on the old sofa watching TV. He asked if Ritchie was OK. Ritchie said he was and sat at the round table next to the sofa. He found the book they were reading and began to practise. Somehow, reading stories helped him forget what was going on down at the bus stop. The story he was reading was a horror story – it was full of zombies and ghosts. Ritchie didn't find it scary at all.

'Everything all right with you?' asked Jamie.

'Fine,' said Ritchie.

'School OK?' asked Jamie.

'Fine,' said Ritchie.

'You've been down the bus stop a lot. What's going on down there?' asked Jamie.

Ritchie paused for a moment. 'Nothing really,' he said, in the most absent-minded voice he could manage.

Jamie went into the kitchen and cooked up some tea and they watched more TV together. Then they went to bed. It was a quiet evening.

At about two o'clock in the morning, Ritchie was woken by a rattling sound on his bedroom window. Like all the windows in the cottage it was old and wooden and it didn't fit its frame any more. When the wind was up the windows all clattered about in their frames. Sometimes Ritchie thought his might fall out, like a bad tooth. Now it was rattling, but there was no wind.

Ritchie pushed his duvet back and tiptoed across the old rug towards the window. He peered outside, but he couldn't see anything. Or rather, he could see things – shadows and shapes – but couldn't quite make them out. There were no stars; the moon was hidden by thick black clouds. He felt something, though. He felt that there was something out there. Ritchie squashed his nose against the glass and peered out towards the farmyard.

Suddenly a shape bounced onto his window-sill. Ritchie leapt back in horror, covering his face. When he looked again, he could see Woody, balancing in the window-frame, gesturing and shouting for Ritchie to open the window.

Ritchie opened the window and let Woody in. He was in a dreadful state. His green skin was blotchy, his clothes were ripped to shreds, and big blobs of green sweat ran down his face.

'Ritchie got to come now! COME NOW!' said Woody, grabbing Ritchie's hand and pulling him towards the window.

A little later, after putting his clothes on and clambering back out through the window, Ritchie and Woody ran down the Winding Lane towards the bus stop. Woody was trying to explain but it didn't make much sense. He kept talking about the Spannermen, the magic stone, and the fact that he needed Ritchie. But Ritchie couldn't work out why.

They reached the bus stop. The road was quiet and dark. The sky was black and the night air was heavy and damp. It was almost impossible to see anything.

'Look,' said Woody triumphantly.

Ritchie couldn't see anything. It was too dark. Woody pulled Ritchie by the hand nearer the gate, near the hole where the stone once was.

'There,' said Woody, pulling Ritchie's hands forward until they touched the stone. Huge and black, Woody had positioned the stone a few meters away from the bus stop. Nearby the singed black crow watched, camouflaged by the night.

'I kept it. I hid it and I kept it and now I've put it here, next to Ritchie's magic bus stop,' said Woody proudly.

'You brought me out of bed to see this?' asked Ritchie. 'This is just a big old stone – it's not magic, it's got no special powers, you just think it has. It's just the biggest stone I could see at the time.'

'No,' said Woody. 'You isn't joking about a thing like this. Even if you say you is. Woody knows the difference between joking, pretending, not telling the truth and lying. You is playing with Woody, you is a pretender.'

'I'm not, Woody,' pleaded Ritchie. 'This is just a big stone. And that hole next to it, where you must have hidden it is … is where it came from. It's just a big old lump of rock.'

'You're telling me,' said Woody. 'And it's magic.'

Ritchie clutched his head with his hands. 'How many times do I have …'

'Anyway,' interrupted Woody. 'This isn't the reason why I brought you here.'

'Really?' said Ritchie.

'No. Not this …' said Woody, tapping the stone with his foot, 'those.' Woody pointed past the gate down the field.

Ritchie strained his eyes, but he still couldn't see anything. He could smell something, though – it reminded him of the metalwork lab in school, blackened steel and oil.

'Spannermen are all over. Woody's been digging

and pulling that stone around all day to keep away from them. Now he's tired. Now he can't move the stone a blinkin' step further. Woody can't move the stone no more.'

Ritchie still couldn't see what Woody's problem was. Then he got it.

There was a distant cry, like a sergeant major ordering his troops. It rang out across the field and suddenly a new sound filled the air: the clanking, grinding sound of rusty metal on metal, the sound of armour on the move, the grinding, wrenching noise of metal on metal. Torches were lit, and now Ritchie could see that this was a problem of gigantic proportions. An army of orange-red, rusty metal knights began to step forward across the field, their heavy clunking feet pounding the grass into mud.

'They want the stone,' said Woody helpfully.

Ritchie watched in horror as thousands of metal shapes clanked and groaned up the field towards them, flashes of flame bursting through patches of light as the Spannermen archers pulled back their metal longbows with piano wire strings. When they released them they twanged together, creating an eerie out-of-tune chord. Arrows began to flick past them, clattering into the side of the stone.

'Woody!' shouted Ritchie. 'What have you brought me here for? You'll get us killed!'

Woody took Ritchie's hand and whispered: 'Ritchie is Woody's friend, he'll help him fight the Spannermen.'

Ritchie could see the Spannermen more clearly now. Half scrap metal, half knights in armour, they looked like old broken cars with washing machine arms and legs. Some carried rusty swords, others axes, and others held lengths of metal pipe with rusty nails smashed through them.

Ritchie looked around desperately for something to defend themselves with. He pulled Woody into the bus stop as the arrows fired up by the Spannerman rattled against the toughened glass. Ritchie picked up a few stones from the floor, the ones he used to play with. He gave Woody a handful.

'What do I do with these?' he asked.

'Throw them,' yelled Ritchie, and together they darted in and out of the bus stop, throwing stones down at the Spannermen. But the stones didn't stop them; they just pinged off the rusty old armour without even denting it. Occasionally they'd hit a finger or a foot and it would fly off.

All that happened was that the Spannerman stopped, groped around for the missing part, and re-attached it using a spanner, nuts and bolts. The Spannermen had perfected the art of self-repair. They seemed to be completely indestructible.

Ritchie turned and looked at Woody. Small, green and panic stricken, he realised that Woody really did think Ritchie could help him, and he understood that Woody genuinely believed the big stone he had picked out of the field boundary held special powers. Above them they could hear the crow squawking and cawing as the Spannermen drew closer. Without thinking, Ritchie jumped up and pulled himself up to the roof. He stuck a hand out and grabbed the crow, pulling it down and into the safety of the bus stop.

'Stay here,' shouted Ritchie to the crow and Woody.

Then he rushed to the field and pulled Shemi to the bus stop. At least they'd be safe for a few more minutes. Ritchie could hear the crack of metal and the grinding and whirring of spanners. Now he had to think quickly – the only preparations he'd made for the defence of the bus stop were slip trenches near the gate, a few piles of stones and, of course, his sticks, the ones he played land-mines with.

'OK,' ordered Ritchie. The sheep, the crow and Woody looked up at him. 'Shemi and Woody, get down in the trench and use the stones; crow, take the sticks and bomb them. When I give the word, fall back to the big stone. That will be our castle.'

Woody and Shemi scuttled off, the crow picked up sticks and started dropping them on the Spannermen. They slowed down the advance, but they couldn't stop the tide.

Ritchie ran down the field in the shadows. He grabbed at the Spannermen and pulled them over with his bare hands, dodging their swiping blades. But there were too many of them. Gradually Ritchie and the others were driven back until they were cornered in the bus stop.

Ritchie looked at Woody. He was breathless, hands on knees, gasping for air. 'What are we going to do Ritchie?' he puffed. 'This is crazy.'

Shemi's chin slid from side to side as if to say: 'He's got a point.'

'Fall back,' yelled Ritchie.

They charged out of the bus stop and clambered to the top of the stone. Finally, Ritchie, Woody and

Shemi were surrounded, kicking back the clanging blades of the rusty arms of the Spannermen. Above them the crow circled, squawking at the top of his voice.

'It's no good,' shouted Ritchie. 'I can't hold them back much longer.'

Woody began to cry as he kicked back at the Spannermen with his green feet. 'Don't make the Spannermen win,' he blubbed. 'I don't want to be eaten, I don't want to lose the stone to these dustbins.'

Ritchie looked up at the crow. It came to him in a flash – he knew what to do. He shouted his instructions to the crow and instantly it flapped off. Then Ritchie remembered something else. He felt something in his pocket and pulled it out. It was the pearly stone the Woolly Woman had given him. She'd told him to use the little stone if he ever got into serious trouble. He could see the Spannermen all around the stone, hauling themselves up the sides, their eyes blazing inside their metal helmets. Trouble didn't get any more serious than this.

'Here goes,' yelled Ritchie, and he threw the Woolly Woman's stone at the Spannermen. There was an explosion and the Spannermen flew backwards, away from the stone.

'Blinkin' marvellous,' shouted Woody.

The Spannermen wavered; they grabbed their missing arms and legs and began tightening them. It didn't seem to matter where things went: three arms, four legs, two heads, hands sticking out from their chests, all with little spanners tightening them up. When they were ready they began to close in again, moaning and groaning like heaving ships.

Ritchie looked around desperately; there was no sign of the crow. Shemi raised his eyes skywards as if to say that now there really was no way out.

But as the Spannermen re-formed and advanced, climbing on top of each other like a sea of rusty crabs so that they were almost level with the top of the stone, Ritchie saw what he wanted to see.

A ghostly looking sky-blue Williams Brothers bus was speeding down from the First Hill and out of the night. Ritchie could hear the big Firestone tyres screeching on the tarmac. Inside, he could see Doc Penfro at the wheel, Kid Welly, Mrs Penfold, Rhiannon, and seat after seat filled with Scaries, wizards with bus passes, druids with ancient spell books, and creatures from the lakes, springs, wells and mountains. As the bus drew closer, Ritchie caught the occasional flash of the crow's wing as it caught the headlights from the bus. The crow had taken the message and brought reinforcements. From the Winding Lane Annie appeared on her bike. She screeched to a halt, knocking over a Spannerman with her back wheel and rushing towards the beleaguered stone, before smashing off more Spannermen with a stick.

'I couldn't sleep,' she shouted. 'And then I heard the noise from down here – I knew it must be you.'

'Nice one, Annie,' yelled Ritchie, holding his hand out and pulling her up to the top of the stone. 'Now you've got yourself surrounded.'

Ritchie urged Shemi and Woody to keep going. Shemi rammed the Spannermen with his head. Ritchie wrestled them with his bare hands and Woody used his spade-like hands as hammers to knock them back.

The bus sped closer. It was the number 37 country bus from the depot, just about visible in the gloom of the night. The crow sat on the roof, squawking at the top of its voice. The bus screeched to a halt and Doc Penfro hit the door button. The passengers poured out. Kid Welly and Mrs Penfold ran at the Spannermen, with Mrs Penfold whacking them with a black umbrella and Kid Welly throwing them over his shoulders with his bare hands. But there were others, too: creatures Ritchie had never met before. Some were in human form: witches, wizards and bards from the hills exchanging spells. Others weren't people at all but unicorns, fauns, griffins and werewolves.

They all laid into the Spannermen. At first the metal knights stood their ground, tightening their joints and fighting back. The noise was terrific, like an out of control engine exploding across a power station at the same time as a roar from a huge football crowd. Then, as if from nowhere, came the tactical masterstroke – the air strike. Ritchie recognised the smell first – the sharp, dry scent of freshly cut coal. He smiled. He knew his request for air support had been granted, the sonic boom shattering the night sky into a thousand pieces as it echoed across the hills, down the cliffs and out into the ocean. It spread out across the world.

Mrs Penfold's dragon, Bertie, smashed the Spannermen with firebombs. Now they were in trouble. They clung onto the stone for a few more seconds, but soon the rusty creatures were falling back in disarray, tumbling down the hill as Doc Penfro, Kid Welly and all the others from the bus charged again and again.

Woody raised his hand as high as he could. 'Blinkin' give me six, Ritchie,' he cried.

Ritchie slapped Woody's hand. He hadn't noticed that Woody had four fingers and two thumbs on each of his shovel-like hands. Even Shemi seemed impressed; he stopped chewing. Ritchie had just won a battle – a battle between creatures most human beings had forgotten could exist. Ritchie, who thought he had no special powers at all, had just sent an army of thousands of Spannermen packing. And if the stone wasn't special to him before, Ritchie was starting to feel that it was special now. It had become special.

Ritchie leaped back up on top of the stone to join Annie, raising their fists in triumph. There was a huge cheer from his followers, too. From the ditches, from the air, from all around he could hear people shouting, 'Ritchie, Ritchie, Ritchie has saved our stone!'

Annie waved her stick and shouted at the top of her voice: 'We've won, we've won.'

Then Ritchie noticed the lights and the sirens. He could see police cars and fire engines approaching from both directions – that meant as far away as St Davids. The noise and the explosions had obviously disturbed the peace – seriously. He glanced up the Winding Lane. His dad, Annie's dad and his dogs were marching down the lane with torches.

He yelled his final instruction to his bus load of spirits: 'Hide – now!'

In an instant Ritchie's army of misfits disappeared. Some, like Woody, dived into the hedges, others, like Mrs Penfold and Rhiannon, used their magic and vanished. The more human ones, like Doc and Kid, used their skills, as they were just very good at getting out of the way; they'd been practising for thousands of years.

When his dad reached the stone upon which Ritchie and Annie were standing, there was nobody left. There was just the stone, the bus stop and above their heads, the indistinct outline of a bus being towed into the night sky and back to its depot by a powerful little dragon called Bertie.

'What's going on, Ritchie?' asked Jamie as Annie Bike's dad arrived with his dogs and his shotgun.

Ritchie looked around him; he didn't know what to say. Quietly, he and Annie climbed down from the stone.

The police arrived. They wanted to know about the explosion, the fact that people all over the area had rung up to complain about low-flying military jets causing sonic booms to rattle their windows and wake their pets.

They all wanted to know what Ritchie and Annie had seen. In the end he had to tell them, and of course they didn't believe him.

'Where did this big stone come from?' asked one police officer, kicking the stone suspiciously with his shiny black boot.

'Never noticed that before,' muttered a fireman, sniffing the air. 'Can I smell a gas leak?'

'It's funny what you don't see when you become too familiar with a road,' said an ambulance driver, joining the police officer at the stone. 'I could have sworn this thing wasn't here last week.'

18 Roxy

'WHERE DID you get this stone from?' asked Detective Sergeant Watkin. He scratched his grey beard, pushed his shoulders back and glared across the table at Ritchie. 'It weighs an estimated 37 tonnes, and the strange thing is, it seems to be getting heavier.'

Ritchie lowered his head. He mumbled something to his dad sitting next to him.

'Chuffin' heck, boy,' shouted his dad. 'Speak up to the officer or I'll lamp you.'

The social worker sitting next to Jamie raised her eyebrows.

The solicitor sitting next to her frowned as her pen sped across the pages of her notebook.

Detective Sergeant Watkin spoke again, slowly. 'That won't be necessary, unless you want to be put on a charge too?' he drummed his fingers on his big round belly.

'I didn't mean it,' said Jamie. 'He's just a dipstick with his tall stories. You'll never get nothing serious ... nothing "real" out of him. He reckons that that bus stop is some kind of cosmic intersection.'

Jamie turned to Ritchie, putting his arm around him. 'Please, Ritchie. I'm not really mad with you. I'm just interested. We're all just interested. Have you any idea where that chuffin' big enormous stone by your bus stop has come from?'

Ritchie looked around at all the faces. They didn't look mean. He sighed and nodded his head. He'd tell them truth. Everyone sighed.

'Well done, Ritchie,' said Jamie, patting his back.

'It was a troll,' said Ritchie.

'An internet troll?' asked the social worker, almost hopefully.

'A green one,' said Ritchie, 'with green skin, different coloured eyes and two thumbs on each hand ...'

Sergeant Watkin stood up and thumped his forehead with the palm of his hand. The social worker scribbled. Ritchie hung his head.

'That's enough!' shouted Jamie, shoving his

chair back and pulling Ritchie to his feet. 'If the boy said he saw a troll, that's good enough for me. Ritchie's a good kid and he doesn't lie. So you lot can leave him alone. Now, can we go home now or are you going to arrest us?'

Sergeant Watkin waved his hand towards the door and Ritchie and Jamie marched off.

After the interview they had a meeting to decide what to do. They wanted to know why Jamie had let Ritchie out so late at night and why he played at the bus stop all the time. They wanted Miss Croons to say what he was like at school. They even asked Annie Bike about Ritchie. The only person they didn't ask about Ritchie was Ritchie himself.

The children at school laughed at Ritchie, especially Connor Collins, Psychic and Delaney. They called Ritchie 'Mad Boy' because he went out at night and climbed stones. Only Annie hung around with Ritchie. She'd meet him at the bus stop and they'd talk about what had happened. She told Ritchie that she'd said to everybody that he was telling the truth, but that they didn't believe her either.

There was one good thing for Ritchie, though. On the day when he was supposed to pay the Collins gang their tenner, he didn't pay. He told Connor that he didn't have the money, even though Mrs Penfold had given him a tenner. The Collins gang cornered Ritchie at break time behind the science block. They said they'd beat him up, but somehow, after the incident with the Spannermen, the supersonic dragon and the battle of the Blue Stone, Ritchie didn't feel scared. So when Delaney shoved him he shoved Delaney back, when Psychic tried to punch him, Ritchie swayed back and landed one straight between Psychic's eyes, and when Collins said he'd follow Ritchie home and get him there, Ritchie laughed and said that Collins would end up at the bottom of the hole where the stone came from, with the stone on top of him. Ritchie said that *they* were the ones who'd better look out in future. It didn't stop them calling him 'Mad Boy', but they never bothered him for money again.

Gradually, other people seemed to want to talk to Ritchie because they were interested in him and what he had to say. It wasn't just kids at school, either. The enormous stone, standing next to its even bigger hole, next to the bus stop, became, if not a tourist attraction, a thing to stop and see – if you weren't in a rush. As the weeks passed, Ritchie found himself being interrupted from his games at the bus stop, not by Woody or Shemi or the silky-voiced Scaries, but by real people who would pull up next to the bus stop, step out of their cars, take a selfie of themselves by the stone and drive off.

Sometimes, as if they had to check that the twenty-foot stone next to the bus stop was the right one, they'd ask Ritchie as he played with his pebbles: 'Is this the stone?'

'Too right,' Ritchie would say. 'It's not magic, though. It got there by accident.'

There was even an article on page nine of the local newspaper. 'Council can't explain Big Stone,' was the headline. It was all about how the man in charge of looking after the roads couldn't say why his men had dug the hole and pulled the stone up. 'According to our records,' he said, 'it's a mystery.'

Not even the Williams brothers from Williams Brothers Buses could shed any light on the matter. 'I can assure you that a stone like that wouldn't even fit in one of our buses,' they said.

However, as the months passed, fewer and fewer people came by the bus stop. The stone – as big as a dinosaur – and its hole – as big as a dinosaur house – became Annie and Ritchie's secret.

'It's as if,' said Annie one day, 'because people don't understand it they can't see it.'

That was the day the Social Worker came to visit.

Ritchie's dad had been really worried and he'd cleaned the whole house from top to bottom. Ritchie spent the tenner in the supermarket on furniture polish, dusters and floor cleaner so that whole place shone like it had never done before. Jamie had complained, as he scrubbed the floors and polished the windows, that he didn't need a Social Worker poking her nose into his business – especially one called Roxy.

'What kind of name's that?' he moaned. 'I can't take orders off someone called Roxy.'

When Roxy arrived Ritchie got his dad to make coffee for her. It wasn't so bad. She just wanted to make sure Ritchie was all right. And as far as Roxy could see, he was. She told Jamie that Ritchie was just very imaginative; she said that his daydreaming should wear off as he grew older and that it was nothing to worry about. She was impressed with the way Jamie helped Ritchie read. She said she thought their cottage was lovely and told them that Mrs Croons at school had said that Ritchie was making real progress with his reading.

When she was leaving, Roxy noticed something on the table by the front door. She picked up one of Jamie's old tapes.

'You like Elvis?' asked Jamie. 'I …'

'Wow,' said Roxy, turning the tape around in her hand. 'This is so retro. How cool is that? Have you got lots of them?'

'Got 'em all,' replied Jamie, 'I …'

But she interrupted him again. 'I love stuff like this – old cassettes and vinyl. I can't stand Elvis, though. I prefer happy music.'

Ritchie looked up at Jamie. Jamie's face went through a strange transition. He was just about to frown and say that Elvis was the best, the King, that he did loads of happy music, when he remembered the song. Ritchie watched Jamie mouth the words – 'Are you lonesome tonight?' – then he shook his head. He banged it with the palm of his hand. 'No you're right,' he said. 'I like all kinds of music. Don't I, Ritchie?'

Ritchie nodded, although he'd never heard anything else but Elvis.

After the Social Worker left Jamie turned to Ritchie and said with a smile: 'She's quite nice, that Roxy.'

Everything seemed to be getting back to normal, or rather, better than back to normal, because 'normal' before wasn't very good at all. In fact, thought Ritchie, everything was different. He'd made friends at school, nobody bullied him any more, his reading was getting better, his dad stopped drinking so many cans of beer, and Roxy gave him loads of new music so he didn't have to listen to Elvis all the time.

But one thing haunted Ritchie. It was the thing that showed that Ritchie and Annie were right. It was the thing that held them together. It was in front of everybody's eyes. It was as big as a bus and yet, strangely, not many people saw it. It was the stone. If anything, thought Ritchie, as he waited for the school bus, the stone was getting bigger – towering over the bus stop, blocking the sun whilst the big hole next to it filled with rainwater and dead things.

19 The King

PERHAPS BECAUSE nobody knew where it came from, and maybe because it wasn't doing any harm, people stopped talking about the stone from nowhere. It could have been because they didn't like being unable to explain where it had come from and how it had appeared. If a stranger asked about the huge stone standing by the lonely bus stop, they said that it was a 'standing stone', then changed the subject. Soon it seemed to everyone that the stone had always stood there, on that spot.

Everyone except Ritchie.

Now Ritchie tried to keep away from the bus stop. He tried to arrive almost exactly when the bus pulled in and, if the bus was late, he'd wait on the other side of the road at the entrance to the Winding Lane. He'd never go *into* the stop to play with his pebbles. Some days he'd come down the lane, sit on the grass verge opposite and look at the bus stop, the stone, the hole and watch the crow flitting between them, wondering what they all meant. He'd remember Woody, and he'd stare at Shemi – keeping his distance down in the field – and try to remind himself that what he knew wasn't just a dream. The stone proved it.

So did Annie.

One evening, as the summer came to an end, Annie joined Ritchie at the Winding Lane and they both sat in the long grass, watching the bus stop.

'It changes every day. It's getting bigger,' said Annie.

'Maybe that's OK,' said Ritchie.

'It's *not* OK,' said Annie.

'I know,' said Ritchie.

They both stared at the stone.

'What d'you think is going to happen?' asked Annie.

'Dunno,' Ritchie said, studying the huge, dark stone, towering high over the bus stop.

'It's like a massive finger,' said Annie, 'pointing up at the sky.'

Ritchie and Annie looked up at the slate grey sky.

'It's cold,' said Ritchie with a shiver. 'Cloud's too low to see any jets.'

'Do you think they're watching – Woody and all the others?' Annie asked.

Ritchie nodded. 'They're all here, hiding in the hedges, digging underground, hanging in the air – and we're doing the same thing. We're no different to them. Watching a stupid bus stop.'

The crow flew from the roof of the bus stop to the stone and sharpened its beak on it.

'Nuts, isn't it?' said Annie. 'Come on. I'll give you a lift on my bike.'

Ritchie didn't want to go. He couldn't stop thinking about the bus stop. He knew something was going to happen. He could feel it. 'It's cold,' he said. A chilly wind had sprung up, blowing down off the Old Mountains.

'It's not summer here any more,' said Annie, 'so get on my bike. I'm not leaving you out here all evening watching an empty bus stop. That's a crazy thing to do.'

Ritchie didn't want to go, but he jumped on the back of her bike and let her ride up the lane, because he didn't want to worry Annie. The truth was, every day, every night, whether he was awake or asleep, all he could think about was the bus stop. Once, the bus stop had been the only place where he felt happy. Now, it was the only place that made him sad. Except it was worse than sad. The place made him feel frightened – scared deep down to the bottom of his heels. The power of the stone, the bus stop and the story frightened Ritchie. He couldn't get the place out of his head. He'd dream about the bus stop, about the Spannermen and the Scaries, and about Woody. He'd wake up in cold sweats thinking about the King and how he wanted to destroy the universe. He'd check outside his window to find out if there was a troll curled up on the sill. The worse thing was the song. It filled his dreams and his days with fear. Even though his dad hadn't played Elvis for weeks, and he'd certainly not sung it, Ritchie kept hearing the song. He'd wake up in the middle of the night, shivering with fear, hearing Elvis singing, 'Are you lonesome tonight?'

Of course he couldn't tell anyone. But Ritchie would even find himself singing the song – as if he liked it. He hated it.

'The stone means that what we saw really happened,' said Annie.

Ritchie thought for a while.

It was a Sunday, AWOL day. Jamie and Ritchie had been to town to meet Roxy for Sunday lunch in the General Picton. On the way back home, Ritchie and his dad had spotted Annie Bike sitting on the grass at the end of the Winding Lane, watching the bus stop.

'She's a funny lass,' said Jamie, as he slowed, 'watching the bus stop like that. I suppose you'll be joining her?'

Ritchie nodded. He stepped out of the car and sat down next to Annie. She didn't acknowledge Ritchie; they both watched in silence. Ritchie sensed something. He looked up the road. He could see a sky-blue bus sliding along the Second Hill. It was Mr Dickinson driving the 437 for Cardigan, the only Sunday service. He elbowed Annie.

The oncoming bus drew their attention. It seemed to be moving painfully slowly. As it rolled down the First Hill, Ritchie could see that there was something odd about it. Perhaps the day was unusually bright, but the bus seemed to be bluer than unusual – it was bright and shining, like a precious stone. Annie nudged Ritchie and they stared intently as the bus approached the stop by the stone with the crow on top.

The crow let out a cry. It had never done that before.

They could see a passenger on the bus, wanting to get off at their stop.

Ritchie stared as Mr Dickinson pressed the breaks and began to slow. His mouth went dry as the shimmering blue bus slowed and slowed until it seemed to be travelling at the speed of a snail. Neither Ritchie nor Annie could take their eyes off the bus. It consumed them, it filled the road with its hissing breaking diesel-filled slowness. Ritchie felt Annie's hand on his. He grabbed it.

He looked at Annie, her eyes were wide with fear, as if she knew something really bad was going to happen. He could hear the hiss of air breaks. He wished the bus wasn't slowing down. He wished it was getting faster. But Mr Dickinson was slowing down, carefully, methodically, safely.

'This is it,' muttered Ritchie.

'I know,' said Annie, shivering. 'Now it's cold.'

The sky slipped into shadow as dark clouds cut off the light. The sea bubbled green and grey, the fields were grey, the stone was almost black.

The blue bus stopped with a sigh. Annie and Ritchie heard the hydraulic doors hiss open and the smack of feet hitting the gravel. But they couldn't see the passenger from their side of the road. Then Mr Dickinson pulled off with a wave and revealed him – standing inside the stop, reading the timetable, moving outside, surveying the fields, touching the stone. A tall man, with thick black hair, his eyes hidden by huge sunglasses, stepped in huge boots towards them. His clothes were ridiculous. He was wearing a shiny silver suit, with huge bell-bottom trousers and a collar turned up high so that it touched the back of his head.

Mr Dickinson tooted the horn as his bus disappeared towards town.

The man pointed at Annie and Ritchie. 'Well hello, everybody,' he said, in a thick American accent.

'Elvis!' stammered Ritchie. 'The King of Rock 'n' Roll.'

'That your stone?' asked the stranger, jabbing his finger at the rock.

'Kind of,' replied Ritchie.

'Heard a lot about it,' said the man. 'Let me introduce myself.' The man filled his chest up with air; he must have been about seven-feet tall.

'Elvis is the King,' whispered Ritchie to Annie. The nightmare at the bus stop had just taken an unexpected turn. Ritchie shivered as he realised that Elvis had haunted him – on cassettes in the car, everywhere he went with dad – it was always Elvis. Whenever anything went wrong, Elvis was there. The song pounded through his head. 'Are you lonesome tonight?'

'I'm the King,' said the man. 'You've been receiving my messages?'

Ritchie nodded sadly as the man shouted at the top of his voice and stepped into the road: 'Are you lonesome tonight?' Then he laughed. The wind picked up and blew the trees. Gorse bushes, dry as dust, shook like rattlesnakes. The King laughed as he clumped towards them; he towered over them as Annie and Ritchie scrambled to their feet.

'Of course,' he added. 'You may also know me by my other name. I don't just do Elvis impersonations, you know.'

'Who are you?' stammered Ritchie.

'The King,' said the King. 'The King of everything. Pleased to meet you, Ritchie, and your friend here – Annie.'

'How does he know?' whispered Annie.

Ritchie felt things change. He was getting used to these sensations – perhaps it was the reason why they called him a One Off. He could feel the hedges and fields fill with eyes, watching their every move. He felt a silence descend on the land. Woody, he knew, was by the gate, staring out from a hole in the ground. Doc Penfro and Kid Welly had rushed up from town and were peeping over from behind the hedge. Mrs Penfold and Rhiannon were standing at the bottom of the hill, viewing them all through a pair of powerful binoculars. Scaries were slipping through every crack in the undergrowth, communicating in that strange, electrifying buzzing way of theirs, and high above them, the distant roar of an aeroplane way above the clouds was, in fact, the sound of the Mrs Penfold's dragon, Bertie, steaming around the stratosphere, surveying the situation. Shemi the sheep stuck his head through the gate. And there were others, new ones, filling the shadows with more presence.

This was the King. The master of the universe. This was the end of the world. The King could take the stone and end it all.

'You know who I am?' asked the King.

'You're the King,' said Ritchie.

'Too right I am, boy,' said the King, moving towards the standing stone. 'Why, I've a mind to snuff you out like candlelight. Have you any idea how hard I've been looking for this stone?'

'No,' said Ritchie.

'Oh I think you do,' said King, shining in his silver suit. 'I've been looking for the missing Blue Stone for almost five thousand years, and you've been keeping me from it for exactly the same amount of time. You're the One Off who kept it back in the first place – well, your little act of defiance has come to an end now.'

The King strode over to the stone and put his hand on its side. 'And now you've lost. This is the afternoon when creation will finally end.' He rested the palms of his hands on the stone. 'I can feel the power,' he screamed. 'Can you?'

The King's voice rolled around the countryside causing stones to clatter against one another.

Ritchie nodded sadly. The power was big

and it was bad. Now the stone looked as black as coal.

The King laughed, he spread his arms out wide. 'I am so sick of this place. And so fed up with you lot,' he pointed at Ritchie and Annie.

Ritchie stepped out into the road. Annie gasped. She was used to Ritchie doing mad things, but this seemed ridiculous. He couldn't possibly have worked out what to do.

'Me and Annie?' Ritchie asked. 'What have we done to hurt you?'

The King laughed. 'I mean everyone and everything. What makes you think I care about you? With this stone I can get rid of the lot of you.'

The King turned his back on Ritchie and strode to the stone. 'Magnificent,' he said. 'Not as blue as I'd expected, but nonetheless magnificent.' The King laughed, throwing his head back. His voice thundered across the land and the foaming sea.

'It's the wrong one,' said Ritchie.

The King looked down at Ritchie. His sunglasses twitched. 'How do you know what stone I want?' he asked, adjusting his sunglasses.

'You're trying to finishing everything off – you need the magic Blue Stone,' said Ritchie.

'I do indeed,' agreed the King. 'I need the stone that will give everyone the blues.'

'That's not it,' said Ritchie. 'That's just a big rock; it's not the Blue Stone. I only picked it because it was so big. Can't you tell? Don't your hands tell you this isn't the stone?'

The King pushed his hands around the stone, feeling every bulge and knock. Ritchie was right – the stone was dead.

Annie's eyes widened like saucers. She stepped out into the road and joined Ritchie. Ritchie could see Woody peeping out of the ground now, and Doc Penfro and Kid Welly had joined Shemi the sheep by the gate.

'The magic Blue Stone is in that hole,' said Ritchie, pointing to the hole. The King walked to the hole, then, with a little difficulty, he scrambled down, his platform boots slipping on the loose earth. He muttered about the amount of trouble he was going to unleash on the world when he found the missing Blue Stone as he scrambled about in the slush at the bottom of the hole.

The wind blew up and hailstones the size of marbles began bouncing on the tarmac. Ritchie and Annie edged closer to the stone. Ritchie knew that this was the moment, the moment when he really could save the world and get rid of all the bad stuff. The King bent down to look at the bottom of the hole. He poked the mud with a stick. The wind was blowing so hard he and Annie had to struggle to shelter behind the stone.

'The Blue Stone is down there, at the bottom of the hole,' yelled Ritchie.

'Where?' screamed the King, filling with rage.

Black storm-clouds sped across the hills. Twisters and waterspouts flared up in the swirling sea. Flashes of lightning slit the sky as thunder boomed out across the world.

Then Ritchie leant on the stone at the top of the hole and pushed with all his might.

It moved. Annie joined him and they both pushed.

'Push!' shouted Annie over the rattle of hail and the roar of the storm.

'I *am* pushing,' yelled Ritchie.

The hail turned to rain and road became a river. But still they pushed the standing stone and, loosened by the water, it slid.

Slowly, silently, it toppled back into the hole. Ritchie saw the King turn just as the rock fell. For a split second he thought he saw the King transform, first into a black butterfly with silver spots, to try to flap his way out of the hole, and then into a beetle, to scurry away. But whatever shape the King took, it was too late; he was locked in the hole. There was no sound after the stone had thudded to the ground – the rock covered the King like a cork in a bottle. In an instant the storm vanished.

Ritchie watched as Woody, Doc, Kid and all the others left, slipping away through the hedgerows. He smiled.

'Blinkin' well done,' muttered Woody as he scurried away.

Ritchie and Annie walked to the bike; they began to push it home.

Ritchie looked at Annie. 'Don't mention this to anyone,' he said as light flooded out across the countryside.

'OK,' said Annie. 'They'd never believe us anyway. Is he dead?'

'No, I don't think so,' said Ritchie, 'but he'll be stuck down there for quite a while.'

20 Two Weeks Later

RITCHIE WALKED down the Winding Lane, his tongue touching the red sweet, which he rolled around his mouth. When he reached the end of the lane he was surprised to find a yellow digger parked just next to the bus stop. He trotted over to see what the two men in reflective yellow jackets and orange trousers were up to.

The crow watched, its blue-black feathers fully recovered from partial incineration. Shemi, nose pressed through the gate, stared. Annie Bike watched, resting on her handlebars by the bus stop.

'The men from the council have come to tidy up the hole,' explained Annie. 'Smooth it off properly, so no one knows it's there.'

Ritchie rolled the sweet around in his mouth; it reminded him of the stone in the hole, the one plugging the gap between the King and the world. He smiled at Annie as he joined her.

'Good job,' he muttered. 'I'm glad it's over.'

Annie nodded as the men worked. One was tall, the other was shorter and fat. He had a brown moustache and sad brown eyes. The tall one stepped into the digger and started shifting earth into the hole. The short one lent on his shovel and gave instructions.

As the earth trickled down over the huge rock, slowly making it disappear, Ritchie wondered if he really was looking at the magic Blue Stone and whether he and Annie would become the last people on earth who knew where it was.

Ritchie's bus arrived and Annie pedalled off to school. 'I bet I get there before you,' she shouted. It was the number 24, still on the 971 route. Gloria was driving. She welcomed Ritchie with her usual smile and he sat down behind her.

As they drove away, Ritchie turned and watched the men with digger. The man on the shovel raised a hand and waved. He seemed to be laughing. Or was he just shouting at his mate on the digger to get on with it? The stubble on his chin looked like black pepper on rice pudding.